SHADOWS OF DAMASCUS

A novel

by

Lilas Taha

To those who survive
To those who are tired of waiting for an end
To those who want to make their own beginnings

Other Novels by Lilas Taha

Lost in Thyme

Bitter Almonds

Table of Contents

PROLOGUE

YASMEEN

Damascus, Syria
Summer 2006

The seductive fragrance of Damascus roses drifted through the open window and flirted with fifteen-year-old Yasmeen's olfactory senses. The potent flowers in her neighbor's yard delivered the best awakening. She loved beginnings, especially early, mid-summer mornings like these. Stretching across the bed, her imagination raced with possibilities for the promising day.

Thursday. The day her older brother's friends visited and stayed well into the evening. Yasmeen ticked off potential visitors in her head, dashing young university students who loved to talk politics with Fadi. Today, she would do her best to discover the name of the quietest member in the group, the thin one with round-rimmed glasses. On her nightstand, the sketch she worked on during the last visit waited for his name, and more details around the eyes.

Peeling off the covers, she tip-toed to the

window. Lively noises matched her optimistic mood. Nightingales sang greetings. Clanging dishes and pots resonated from surrounding houses beyond high walls. Mothers called out for their daughters to get breakfast ready. Men's deep voices describing fresh fruits and vegetables with tempting traditional phrases drifted above hidden alleys. One vendor claimed his cucumbers were small as baby fingers and likened his ripe apples to a virgin bride's cheeks. Another boasted his plum peaches shed their covers without enticement, and his shy eggplants hid well in a moonless night.

Yasmeen succumbed to the enlivening chaos spilling in from her bedroom window, her own special and personal opening to the world. Tilting her head back, she exposed her face and neck to the sun, allowing its invigorating rays to paint her cheeks.

Today, her mother told her she would be allowed to take a coffee tray into Fadi's room once all his friends arrived. What would she wear? She should tell her best friend Zainab to stop by earlier than usual to go through her wardrobe. She could help her decide. Perhaps one of Fadi's friends would notice her. More than one? Why not?

Draping her arms on the windowsill, she looked at the neighbor's yard, counting the blooming roses, a ritual she performed each morning since the season started. In the north corner of the largest flowerbed, two violet buds grabbed her attention, their delicate petals about to unfold. Once they came to full bloom, their deep purple color would dominate the landscape.

A knock sounded at her door.

"I am awake."

Her father walked in. "Good. We have work to do." He held a hammer in one hand and a couple of boards in the other. "Move aside, Yasmeen." He approached the window.

She stepped away and pointed at the boards. "What do you need those for?"

Her father closed the windowpanes, locked them, placed one board across the frame, and hammered it in place.

"What are you doing?"

"This window is not to be opened again, child."

She could not believe her ears. "Why?"

"Neighbors moved out last night." Her father nailed the second board in place.

"*Mukhabarat* took over their house."

ADAM

Baghdad, Iraq
Summer 2006

M4 Carbine rifle ready, Sergeant Adam Wegener scanned the street, skimming from window to rooftop. Nerves on edge, his neck and shoulder muscles strained to keep him focused. His heart thumped against his ribs.

Patrol leader Lieutenant Clifton moved his troop with caution through the street, Adam's fire team at the rear. They'd done street sweeps many times before, but this one was different. Something was not right. Apprehension took hold of his insides and squeezed tight with every step.

Adam turned and walked backwards a few steps, establishing eye contact with Corporal Scottsdale. He nodded at the big guy's expressionless face, assurance at having Big Scott cover his back. He checked on the other two members of his team trailing his left, Corporals Andrews and Bradley, and faced forward again.

The neighborhood seemed unnaturally quiet. No children walked to school, no laundry hung outside windows on this breezeless day, not even alley cats explored the overflowing garbage containers.

From a corner of his eye, he caught a movement in one of the windows. Wood shutters slammed closed against the windowpane.

A loud boom burst the air. Adam hit the dirt, his head pounding the pavement. The world went silent. He spat blood mixed with something solid. Parts of his body armor and uniform had been ripped off, along with patches of skin. He rose to his knees, his hands searching for his rifle. Finding it, he clasped the rifle in his arms and crawled. He moved as if swimming in a viscous liquid, not knowing which direction to take. He saw only clouds of smoke.

He screamed the names of the soldiers in his team, not sure if his voice even worked. He couldn't hear a damn thing. His elbow landed on something hard, a boot. He moved his fingers up the leather, across the twill fabric of the pants, until his hands sank in soft flesh and wetness. The man mumbled something, his voice muffled and distant.

"Big Scott, that you?" Adam shouted.

A shower of bullets rang by his side. Helmet gone, he ducked and covered his head. His ears popped from the pressure, jump-starting his hearing.

"Take cover." Big Scott's voice penetrated the sounds of warfare.

He scrambled to his feet, hoisted Big Scott on

his shoulder, and dashed to the nearest house. He kicked the door and threw himself and Big Scott inside. Propping the injured soldier's back to one wall, away from the windows, he snatched the M9 Beretta pistol from the holster mounted on his chest rig and forced it into Big Scott's hands.

"Cover the door."

Rifle raised and ready, he moved from room to room to secure the small house. He entered the kitchen, coming face-to-face with an old woman. Sitting motionless on a wooden chair, hands clasped on the Formica table in front of her, she stared down Adam's raised barrel.

Keeping an eye on the wrinkled, tanned face, he scanned the kitchen. No place for anyone to hide, not even a closet door to check behind.

"Anyone else in the house?"

She held her stare, unflinching.

Adam tried to recall Arabic words he heard Fadi, the interpreter assigned to his patrol unit, say in situations like these. But he couldn't recall a single one.

"Where's your husband?"

The woman blinked. She craned her neck to one side, looking past him toward the front of the house. The white scarf covering her hair slipped down to her shoulders, revealing gray strands pulled back in a tight bun. She lifted the scarf and refastened it under her chin.

His hand shook. He aimed a loaded weapon at a woman the same age as his mother. Hell, she even resembled her.

"Rajul? Rajul?" Was that the right word for man? Why was she so calm?

The only point of entry was the door he came through. He heard heavy movement outside. The sounds of shouting men grew closer. The old mother could yell to alert the insurgents any second. He snatched a towel hanging on a hook to his left, and held his index finger to his lips, motioning for the woman to go with him to the front room.

She followed without uttering a sound.

Adam pointed his weapon for her to sit on the cement floor. He tore the towel into strips and kneeled in front of her.

Big Scott moaned. He slumped to one side, pistol aimed at the door.

"I got you, man. Have to secure the old mother first."

He used a towel strip for her hands and tied another around her mouth.

He turned to Big Scott, got his first aid kit out of a side pocket on his torn pants, and dug for supplies. He applied bandages to Big Scott's bleeding midsection. Keeping pressure on the wound with one hand, he pulled the radio from his pack and reported to his platoon sergeant they were trapped inside one of the houses.

"Damn it, which one?" Lieutenant Clifton's voice crackled.

"Don't know. Scottsdale's injured. It's bad."

"Andrews, Bradley?" The lieutenant screamed back.

"God damn IED was right under them. Can't confirm."

"Second platoon's six blocks away. They're en route and—"

A loud explosion silenced the radio. Cursing, he flung the radio across the room.

"Hang in there, big man. QRF's on the way." There was no way the Quick Reaction Force could come to their rescue if they didn't know where they were.

"How long?" Big Scott's voice came out calm, surprising him.

"Ten minutes." He fumbled with more bandages. Could second platoon make six blocks in ten minutes? It was possible. "Stay with me. Think about that sweet girl you got back home. Sandy, right?"

He slumped beside Big Scott. Sticky stuff on his

back squished. He closed his eyes, hoping to God the sensation resulted from an injury he hadn't yet felt, rather than the blood and flesh of his missing team members splattered all over him. He needed to find a way to signal their location.

Big Scott clamped a charred hand on top of his. "Won't make it."

"The hell you won't. Sandy's waiting for you." He pulled himself to his feet and approached the door. "You'd better not disappoint her." If he opened the door and his patrol didn't spot him, the insurgents would be alerted to their position, and that would be the fucking end. If he didn't do anything, Big Scott would bleed out. He looked back at the corporal. His friend didn't have much time. There was only one thing to do.

"We have to get out of here."

He propped Big Scott on his shoulder and opened the door. Clouds of smoke blocked his view. Using the cover of smoke, he edged his way along the side of the house, unable to see a yard past his face. His foot stumbled over a chunk of cement, and he collapsed against the house, slumping down on the dirty street, overcome by how absurd this mission was.

A clomp of boots on the gritty pavement caught his attention. They were trapped. They could not fade into the concrete, not a car nor a bush to hide behind, and he didn't have time to retrace his way back to the door. He aimed his rifle in the direction of the approaching boots and counted the steps. One man, probably a scout. Shots would draw others.

He slung the rifle across his chest and let it hang. Clamping a hand on Big Scott's mouth, he stifled the soldier's agonized moan. Adam stretched to full height, flattened his back against the wall, and pulled his knife.

Heavy fire erupted around them. Bullets shattered the wall to Adam's left. He hit the dirt again. Big Scott's limp body fell on top of him, pinning him down. Knife gone, he tried to push Big Scott off. Pain shot through his body like electricity. He doubled over and collapsed once more, trapping his rifle under him.

Leather boots slammed right next to his face. He wrapped his hand around the ankle and tried to topple the guy down.

"Don't fight me, Adam. I'm here to helb you."

"Fadi? That you Fadi?"

"Shut ub before zey hear us."

Fadi took hold of Big Scott's shoulders and pulled him into the house. He returned to Adam and dragged him until they were inside. He checked their injuries.

Multiple holes on Adam's left side bled. Big Scott lay flat on his back, praying aloud.

"Clifton knows where you are now." Fadi applied bandages to Adam's leg.

He sucked in a sharp breath and tried to stay alert, his eyelids too heavy to keep open.

Fadi shook his uninjured shoulder. "Do what you always do to stay awake."

Adam opened his eyes. "What?"

"Count, man. Count za bains. Double za number if zey were very bainful, half if zey were minor," Fadi urged in his particular accent.

Adam's mind kicked into counting mode. Shit, was he crazy?

"How'd you know where we were?"

"I heard za insurgents shouting to each ozer." Fadi moved fast to administer the articles in his first-aid kit to Adam's other wounds.

Crunching numbers didn't do much to alleviate his pain, but the process helped him filter through Fadi's heavy accent.

"At first I didn't understand the words they were using for directions," Fadi explained. "Arabic has two words to indicate left. One can mean north, depending on the dialect. I had to get closer to figure it out, and that's when I saw you. Clifton was very mad. Didn't want me to leave the team, but hey, I'm a contract interpreter, not one of his soldiers."

The woman moaned from her corner. Fadi shot his head up and approached her.

"Who did this?"

"Needed to make sure she didn't scream." Adam tried to lift himself on his elbows. He groaned, the full force of deep searing pain setting in.

Fadi untied the woman's mouth, released her hands, and spoke to her, his tone low and gentle.

"She's an old woman, Adam. She's trapped here just like we are. This is her home. No one and nothing is going to drive her out of it. You didn't need to tie her up."

"Not taking any chances."

Scott's praying voice disturbed rather than comforted Adam. He concentrated on breathing. Why couldn't he just pass out and be spared this agony?

The woman placed her hands in her lap, flipped her palms upward and muttered something.

"What's her problem?"

"She's praying," Fadi said.

"I didn't hurt her. See what else you can do for Big Scott before I lose it." Adam found it hard to formulate his words.

Fadi kneeled in front of Big Scott, tore a bag with his teeth, and spread its contents over his gaping wound.

Adam's eyes darted between the old mother and Big Scott. Never hesitant Scott. Never questioning and never smiling either. Were they praying to the same God? Would He listen?

"Tell her I'm sorry I tied her up, will you?"

"*Itlaa barrah balady*," the woman responded to Fadi.

"What the hell did she say?"

"She wants us to leave."

"We wouldn't be here if her people hadn't planted that Goddamn IED. Tell her that." Adam spat blood.

"She meant leave her country."

Darkness closed in on Adam, the bliss of unconsciousness threatening to take over. He closed his eyes.

"I'm okay with that . . ."

CHAPTER 1

A FAVOR

Platteville, Wisconsin
Five years later

A handwritten, old-fashioned note, not an email or even a phone call. Before he opened the envelope, Adam checked the handwriting for a clue to its sender. The writing wasn't familiar. The letter had no return address, only a five-day-old stamp from Turkey.

At the kitchen table in his two-story farmhouse in the late afternoon, he studied the unopened envelope. He ran his fingertips over the name, Adam Wegener, a name he officially adopted as soon as he turned eighteen, right before he joined the army. Wegener was his mother's maiden name, and he decided to use it the day he severed ties with his father. Adam would no longer be a Shipman.

When he came home after his medical discharge from the army, his small circle of friends downsized to one, Jonathan. As for family, his mother passed away and his father lost the privilege the day Adam threw him out. Who cared enough to send him a handwritten letter?

With a heavy heart, he opened the envelope. He read over the slanted handwriting, some words crossed out, as if written in a hurry. He locked on the signature, O.R. Pemssy. He sounded out the name, but it triggered no familiarity. He folded the letter, placed it on the table, and clasped his hands on the wooden surface.

Five years since he left Iraq. These written words threw him headfirst into that time. A stream of images filled the space around him. A slide show of faces, proud soldiers, weapons in hands. Faces twisted in pain, many stamped with the stillness of death that soon followed.

The sun made its final dip behind the horizon. The letter on the table riffled in the light breeze from the window. He picked it up and read it again. The signed name didn't match the face in his head. Big brown eyes, dark thick eyebrows and a matching mustache. Fadi Jabir, the Syrian interpreter with the annoying accent.

Before he shipped off to Germany, Fadi paid him a visit while he lay bandaged and disoriented from morphine in the Army base hospital. His jumbled memories of that visit scattered like pieces of a jigsaw puzzle. He remembered Fadi's face, a painful handshake, and a promise being made. The rest dispersed into emptiness. He owed his life to Fadi, no question about it. But whose signature was this? Who was O. R. Pemssy?

Unfolding his body from the chair, he switched the lights on, and went for a glass of water. Fadi's selfless act invaded his mind many times over the years. Attempts to locate him through army records failed, information blocked by military regulation. Further inquiry led him to the name of the private company that contracted Fadi from Syria to U.S. troops in Iraq, but the company dissolved, and no credible records remained.

Now, he had this mysterious letter in his hands, asking him to start from the beginning, and no way to do a damn thing about it. Exhaling in frustration, he took his cold glass outside to the front porch.

The summer breeze, pregnant with the intoxicating smell of flowering jasmine, took him back to the time he planted the bush with his mother. He must have been seven, and he remembered her excitement when she found it in a nursery. Later, he helped her plant the apple tree in front of her bedroom window, and a couple of years after, the pear tree by the barn.

He collected a few jasmine flowers and went

inside. He filled a small bowl with water and deposited the delicate collection. The fragrance filled the area around him. He walked to the table and thumbed the letter again. How could he reach Fadi?

He flipped the paper to check the backside, nothing. Holding it against the light, he searched for clues, and then dropped the letter, and picked up the envelope.

The Turkish stamp and the date seemed legitimate, nothing more to see in that. He concentrated on the signature, the only thing that didn't make sense.

Adam wrote the words of the signature on separate lines, trying combinations for the letters, comparing them with Fadi's full name. After an hour of futile work, he massaged his stiff neck. He opened his laptop and searched the name in its entirety, then separately. Nothing solid surfaced.

The evening sky melted into night, and his frustration intensified. He pinned the letter on the fridge door with a magnet and paced.

Fadi wanted something. Something dangerous. Otherwise, why the secrecy and the ambiguity, using an alias? He wanted Adam to contact him, so how could he do that? Write a letter? There was no address. Call him? No number. Start from the beginning. Start what? Start counting?

He took a pencil and circled the letters, counting them and assigning numbers in succession. The first O is at number two. The R is either forty-seven on the first line or one on the second line. The P is at number six on the third line. He worked through the script.

The process gave him a number with ten digits starting with area code 216. Was this possible? Did he crack a code? Fadi knew how his crazy mind worked? Knew him well enough to send him a coded number? Why? What was so secretive?

He went online to find which city the area code covered. Cleveland, Ohio. Jumping to his feet, he snatched the phone handset and checked his watch. Past midnight. His fingers hovered over the dial keys. Was it too late to call? What's the worst that could happen? Get cursed at? What if this wasn't Fadi, and the whole thing was a set up? Who would screw with him like that?

He returned the handset and drew back. It couldn't be this urgent if the sender chose a coded letter to contact him. Better wait until morning, when he had some rest and could think clearer.

He headed upstairs. Passing through the living room, he looked around, feeling the emptiness, recalled memories often more bitter than sweet. He stopped in front of the mantle and turned his attention to the framed document above, his grandfather's will, leaving him the farm. About halfway down the paper, one line was underlined. Adam ran his eyes on the typed words out of habit. He committed them to memory years ago. His grandfather explained the decision of passing the farm to Adam instead of his only son in two simple sentences:

Fred Shipman is a bad seed and shall not inherit The Shipman Farm. Full ownership shall be instated with my grandson, Adam Shipman.

Dejected and mentally drained, he moved on to his room, and set his alarm clock to four a.m. He'd use the extra thirty minutes before milking time to go over the letter again, see if he missed anything. Maybe he was taking this coding thing too far. Maybe there was no number there, and he was just as obsessive as he'd always been. And maybe he was on to something, something that would cut through this tedious life of his.

Stretching on his bed, he heard his heartbeat, fast and loud. Too long since he felt this charged. Too damn long since he had something to look forward to when he woke up, anything to make him forget the usual nightly visits of his dead friends.

***

Hot cup of coffee in one hand, phone receiver cradled on shoulder, Adam dialed the phone number at eight thirty the following morning. A decent time. A woman's soft voice greeted him.

"Good morning, ma'am. I'd like to talk to Mr. Pemssy?" He barely contained his excitement.

"Sorry?"

"My name is Adam Wegener," he enunciated his words. "I want to speak to Mr. O. R. Pemssy."

"Wrong number."

Click.

"Damn it." His excitement disintegrated like a popped balloon. He went back to the kitchen table and re-worked the letters again, only to end up with the same number. Frustrated, he crumbled the papers and threw them across the kitchen floor. To hell with this, he'd wasted enough time on this shit. If Fadi wanted something from him, he damned well better call him.

Hungry and angry, he stabbed a slice of toast and smeared it with peanut butter. Tension building in the muscles of his arms, he wanted to throw or break something. Instead, he swallowed the sandwich and went outside to work. Climbing astride his rusty old tractor, he cranked the motor.

Rising heat squeezed sweat from his body like a sponge with no regard to his fragile mental state. His mind crunched numbers without end while he worked. Thoughts of the cool fridge full of icy drinks beckoned him for an early lunch. He abandoned his tractor in the middle of the field, and headed home, discarding his wet shirt on the way. He walked around the kitchen, stomping papers. It felt good and satisfying. As satisfying as the icy Coke he gulped down. Needing to put things in order, he collected the discarded papers. When he reached to crush the envelope, his eyes landed on the Turkish stamp. A surge of excitement gripped his stomach. One more thing he needed to try.

Logging onto his laptop, he searched Turkey's city codes for area code 216. Istanbul on the Asian side. He searched for the country code, then the time difference. Eight hours ahead put it close to nine p.m. in Istanbul.

He dialed the sequence of international code numbers and held his breath while the same ringing tone played with his nerves.

"'Allo?" A man's voice greeted.

"May I speak to Mr. Pemssy?"

"Yust a minute." The man spoke with an

unmistakable heavy accent.

Adam dropped in a chair and closed his eyes in anticipation.

"I see you got my letter," a deep voice said.

"You're the one who sent it? Who am I speaking to?" Eyes wide open now. Could it be Fadi? Damn it, he couldn't remember his voice.

"You know who I am. I can't use my real name. How is zat hib of yours? Giving you trouble?"

Fadi. Same annoying accent. "What the hell is going on?" He gritted his teeth and tried to ignore the mispronunciations. "Couldn't you have given me your phone number in the letter, or called me directly?"

"I didn't know if you still lived at that address, and I didn't want my number to fall in the wrong hands. You're not listed. I knew you liked to count things. That was the best I could come up with."

"I too tried to find you many times. What can I do for you, man? What do you need?" Was there a better way to say he hadn't forgotten Fadi?

"I need a favor. But I can't explain over the phone. Get on a plane and come here as soon as possible."

"You want me to fly to Turkey? You serious?"

"You promised to help if I needed anything, and I do. Desperately."

Adam coughed to steal a moment. What the hell? Fly over there? Could he even afford it? He'd like to help the guy, but this was insane.

"Can't just drop everything and leave. I'll do my best to help you from here if you tell me what you need. Nothing illegal, you should know this upfront."

"I can't tell you, and I can't stay on the line for too long. A life is at stake. Are you in or out?"

Adam was torn. Torn and ashamed to admit he looked for a way out of the promise he'd given years earlier. "Your life?"

Fadi remained silent for a few seconds.

He heard an agonized exhale.

"You're my only hope."

CHAPTER 2

A TRIP

Six hours had passed since Adam boarded the plane heading to Frankfurt. The woman sitting next to him had been in constant movement, sliding in her seat, raising her knees to lock them on the back of the seat in front of her, and twisting her petite body to invade the personal space of her husband or boyfriend.

Adam couldn't imagine himself in place of that poor man, touched nonstop, spoken to, and kissed on his head while trying to read a book. At one point, she deposited her manicured feet on the pages. He needed to distract himself before he extended a helping hand to tighten the woman's seatbelt.

From a pocket in his backpack, he produced the letter that propelled him on this foolish trip, not knowing what Fadi had in store for him. He unfolded the paper and tried to smooth the crinkled page, his eyes skipping over the crossed-out words and the numbers he jotted down during his attempts to figure out where to call.

Dear Adam,

You once told me you owe me ~~your~~ a life because I saved yours. I'm sure I don't need to remind you of ~~that day~~ the details. No one survives ~~that~~ such horror and forgets about it.

~~I have to~~ I'm compelled to ask for the return of that favor. If you remember who I am, you know that asking for payback is not an honorable ~~thing~~ act for me. But for the sake of the people I love, I must. Do what you always do. Start from the beginning and don't delay. Time is crucial.

Your friend,
O. R. Pemssy

He slid the letter back in its envelope and tucked it away again. The flight's final destination was Istanbul with a three-hour layover in Frankfurt.

***

In the Lady Diana Hotel in Istanbul, Adam rolled over in bed. Euphoric voices sang out calls for dawn prayers, waking him from a sound sleep. Jet-lagged and exhausted, he sat on the edge of the bed and tried to orient himself. He'd heard these calls before in Iraq, so they didn't startle him like they did those who heard them for the first time. The singing voices from mosque minarets enticed the sleeping to rise and perform prayers, do a good deed, or make merit of some sort. Even though the calls were not for him, he felt a tug at his chest. He had come here to do a good deed, hadn't he?

An hour later, he stepped out of the hotel's revolving door onto the throbbing streets. Strong Turkish coffee in his mouth and baked pastry aroma accompanied him on his way to the Blue Mosque. Fadi had instructed him over the phone to go to the mosque for a meeting.

The historical district buzzed with activity and noise. Tourists flooded the area of *Sultanahmet* Square with the six minarets of the Blue Mosque dominating its skyline. In the distance, a cascade of smaller domes spilled down from the great central dome. None of the visible exterior was blue. Where did the mosque get its name?

Shop owners spread their precious hand-crafted rugs, ceramic plates, colored scarves and mosaic lanterns on freshly washed pavements, luring people like skilled fishermen drawing in their nets. A joyous atmosphere pulsed in the environment, in the laughing faces and bouncing gaits of both young and old. He joined the crowd in their mood, the positive energy running through him, his earlier nervousness gone, replaced with optimism.

The walk from the hotel took a good forty minutes. His left leg ached with customary pain, sharp throbs traveling in waves from hip to toe. He stood by a huge marble urn on the northern end of the square and leaned on one of the eight columns surrounding it. The urn had a number of faucet-like fixtures scattered around its base.

A teenager wearing a blue tee-shirt with a question mark on his chest approached him. "Can I help you, sir? English? *Français*?"

More young boys and girls wearing the same tee-shirt talked to tourists. He must have the same lost look on his face. "Thank you, I'm waiting for someone."

The young man smiled, handed him an English pamphlet, and walked away. Adam stomped his foot to relieve the pain in his leg and stole another glance at his watch. Too early. To pass the time, he scanned the pamphlet.

The Blue Mosque got its popular name because of the twenty thousand blue tiles that lined the interior of its high ceiling.

He checked his watch again, looked around for a sign of Fadi, and continued reading.

The urn was built in Germany, transported piece

by piece to Istanbul and assembled as a gift to the Sultan in 1900. He looked at the faucets surrounding the urn. Did they still work?

"Adam."

He looked up. Fadi, a couple of feet away, was in a white shirt and dark pants, looking thinner than Adam remembered, his face pale without the dark mustache. Fadi's eyes scanned the crowd, no smile on his face.

Something was wrong, terribly wrong.

Sweat beaded Adam's forehead, and his shirt stuck to his back. Studying a nervous Fadi across the space separating them, he hoped Fadi didn't sense his uneasiness. If he had ever imagined this moment, it was different. A leap forward, a happy embrace and a slap on the back. What he didn't expect was the stillness, this statue-like stance from the man who risked a lot to give him another chance at life. He tried to close the distance.

Fadi backed away, nodded at a little souvenir store on the edge of the square, and hurried toward it.

Adam followed him into the hole-in-the wall shop. Sagging balloon pants of all colors, tee-shirts, leather sandals and knick-knacks for tourists lined the cramped space. Fadi disappeared behind a damask burgundy curtain at the rear of the shop.

A couple of women shoved Adam toward the curtain when they entered the shop behind him. He gave them a questioning look. They ignored him.

"I found them!" The younger of the two sounded excited. "Look here, Annie. Aladdin pants."

"Finally." The older woman neared, pushing him closer to the curtain with her body, tourists looking for bargains. He lifted one corner and looked into a storage space lit by a single light bulb. Fadi's unsmiling face beckoned him. He stepped in and let the curtain fall behind him.

"I'm so habby you made it, my friend," Fadi whispered in his distinguished accent.

Adam took a deep breath and installed that mental filter for Fadi's articulation. Aware of the women on the other side of the curtain, he mirrored Fadi's hushed voice. "I try to keep my promises, but what the hell is going on?"

"There's a private room upstairs. Follow me." Fadi opened a back door. They ascended narrow steps in dim lighting. Adam's shoulder scraped the walls in the narrow passageway. He surveyed Fadi, searching for concealed weapons, the uneasy feeling in his gut growing like a weed. A closet-like door at the top of the stairs opened into a room with decent lighting. Two bare light bulbs dangled on wires from the ceiling. Adam walked in, scanned the area for another exit. No windows. A narrow bed occupied one wall. A wooden chair leaned against the opposite wall; the floor covered by a worn-out rug.

Fadi motioned for him to sit, attempting a smile. "It's safe here."

"Safe from what?" Adam straddled the chair. "Who's after you?"

Fadi lowered his body onto the bed, sluggish, moving like a man who hadn't slept in days.

"*Mukhabarat*, you know? Secret police, regime supporters, mercenaries, take your pick."

Adam recognized the signs of extreme fatigue in Fadi's ghost-like appearance. Eyes bloodshot, lips dry and chapped, sweat circles under his arm pits, he looked beyond haggard. The man was falling apart. "Why don't you start from the beginning? What do the Turks and the secret police want with you?"

"Syrians, not Turks. Haven't you been following the news? The uprising in Syria?"

Fadi's accusatory tone did not sit well with him. He heard the news when the uprising broke out in Syria months ago. Civilians by the hundreds died, women and children were killed. That was the extent of his knowledge. His life was not affected.

He knew no one in Syria.

"How are you involved in any of this, Fadi?"

"Don't say my name." Fadi sprinted to the door and put his ear to the wood. "Don't you understand?"

Adam nodded. Shit. The man was really fucked up. "Walk me through it."

Shoulders hunched, Fadi dragged his feet back to the bed. "I'm one of the underground opposition organizers. From the start. *Mukhabarat* thugs know my name now." Fadi stared into space, making him appear more dead than alive. "They're targeting my family."

"Secret police? They're looking for you here in Turkey?"

"I crossed the northern border two weeks ago, but they have eyes here. They killed two of my uncles in Damascus, kidnapped my father, hoping to pressure me to turn myself in. I can't go back. Not yet." He studied his clasped hands. "You know what they will do to me. Same things they're doing to my father."

Adam knew this all too well, from his time in Iraq. Some outcomes of war weren't tied to geography or specific to a time period. There were actions by fellow soldiers he had witnessed, violations he was helpless to prevent, images he was desperate to erase from his memory. "Not sure what I can do for you."

Fadi lifted his head. "Help me."

"I can probably take you to the U.S. embassy."

"What for?"

"See if they can give you a special visa and get you the hell out of here."

Fadi pulled his body off the bed, a spark in his tired eyes, making Adam regret giving the man hope for something he wasn't sure he could deliver.

"Not me. I want you to get someone else out. My sister."

"She involved with the opposition too?"

"I'm her death sentence. They will go after her to get to me." Fadi turned away and spoke to the wall. "You know what that means, don't you? Those animals taking hold of the young sister of an opposition leader? What they'll do to her? She told me she isn't afraid to die. She doesn't know there are worse things than death."

Adam rubbed the bridge of his nose.

Fadi faced him again, a burst of energy making him look somewhat normal. "Take her away. Just get her out of here. Sooner or later my father and I will be dead, and she will have no one to protect her. Please, that's all I ask."

"What're you saying?"

"You're the only one who can do it. Remember how I helped you?"

"You don't have to remind me of that. But what the fuck can I do?"

"Something. I'm not sure what."

He peered into Fadi's face. Fadi had a plan. He was sure. He obviously didn't want to spill it yet. Shit! What had he gotten himself into? He could have come up with a thousand excuses not to come here. All legitimate. "So, where is she? Istanbul?"

"I left her at the refugee camp on the border. No contact since I got to Istanbul. God help me, Adam, she's barely twenty-one. No telling what they will do to her. For the moment, she's safe with a family friend. *Mukhabarat* thugs don't know she's there, but I'm running out of time. A couple of them were spotted around the camp. We have to get her out."

"We?" Adam looked Fadi hard in the eye. Fadi meant business. The man believed he could help him. Adam cleared his throat. "What about the Turkish authorities? Have you asked for their help?"

"I can't. I'm not supposed to leave the camp, but they wouldn't give me a permit, so I snuck out. If I go to the police, they will just take me back. We will be exposed."

Adam ran his hands through his hair in

frustration. We? What's this *we* shit?

"The camp is guarded by Turkish police, right? Then how the hell can you . . . we get her out of there? I told you, I'm not getting involved in anything illegal."

"Okay, forget the camp. I will figure out a way to sneak her out. All it takes is one corrupt guard. But I can't keep her in Turkey for too long."

He tried to keep his uneasiness with Fadi's hidden plan under control. A knot took hold of his insides. "Then where'd she go?"

Fadi became animated, stepping closer. "With you." His eyes glowed with anticipation. "You have to take her to America. Just keep her safe until this is over."

Holding the top of his chair, he pushed his upper body further back. "What do you mean, take her with me?"

Fadi squatted in front of him. "I have to return, but not until my sister is safe. I know she will be safe with you. You're here. You kept your word. I trust you."

"Wait a minute. I don't think I can get her a visa. It's different for you. You've worked with the U.S. army before. It would be easier in your case to talk them into granting you a temporary stay. But for her, what the hell am I going to say?"

"You can say she's your wife."

He jumped off the chair as if electrocuted. It crashed to the floor, knocking Fadi off balance and on his backside.

"Hold on. Give me a goddamn second, here."

"You can do this," Fadi urged, paused, and briefly closed his eyes. "You don't have a wife, right?" His voice rang with doubt.

"No, I don't have a fucking . . . I'm not married. Don't want to be either." Adam crossed his arms. "Especially not to your sister."

Fadi dragged himself to the wall, bent his knees and hung his head. "All I care about is getting her as far away from here as possible. You must help me." Desperation marked every word.

He paced the small room. "Don't know. I can't think. Look, I want to help, I really do. But that's not the way to go." He stopped, shoved his hands in his pockets and tried to reason. "I can see if I could get some form of protection for you—"

Fadi abruptly shouted back. "*I* don't need protection, s*he* does!" He jumped to his feet and took hold of Adam's shoulders. "They've threatened my cousins in Europe. They *will* find her if she stays here. *You* can protect her. You. Owe. Me."

CHAPTER 3

AN AGREEMENT

Adam waited at the designated meeting point at the Chicago airport and scanned the crowd. He arrived early in case Yasmeen cleared immigration and customs faster than expected. He searched for a woman in a white dress and a blue scarf, his blue tie hanging loose over his white shirt, Fadi's idea of identification. He went over in his head the series of events that led him to this moment, trying not to feel silly in his bright white pants.

A visit to Big Scott at the American Embassy in Germany started the ball rolling. Big Scott pushed Adam's application for a spousal visa through the proper channels in record time, and Yasmeen Jabir was granted entry to the U.S. to join her husband.

Dignity. That was the first word that popped into his head when he saw her. He spotted her as soon as she exited the main doors. An ankle-length white dress moved elegantly with her petite figure, a bright blue scarf draped around her shoulders. Dark hair framed a young face, making Adam doubt he was looking at the right woman. This one seemed much younger.

Head held high, shoulders pulled back, her chocolate eyes struck his for a fraction of a second as she scanned the waiting crowd. Recognition sank in when she brought her eyebrows together and returned her eyes to him. It was obvious she recognized him, and she frowned. How was that for an ego bruise?

He stepped around the roped area where arriving passengers mingled with loved ones and pasted a smile on his face.

"*Marhaba! Ana* Adam Wegener." Proud of himself for the few Arabic greeting words he practiced.

Still frowning, Yasmeen extended her hand, marked by a birthmark the size of an almond. "I know who you are. I am Yasmeen Jabir, of course."

Taken aback, he did not expect her to be fluent in English. Wait a minute, hadn't Fadi said she was a college graduate? And wasn't he told, during his training years ago, it was unacceptable for men and women to shake hands in her culture? Why was he so confused? He was her legal husband, after all. He took her hand but didn't fold his fingers around it. Let her do what she wanted with it.

Yasmeen held rather than shook his limp hand

and released it with an awkward shove.

Damn! He'd seem like an absolute wimp to her now. He reached for her suitcase. "This all the luggage you have?"

Yasmeen nodded, softening her frown. "Can you direct me to the water circuit, please?"

She didn't seem to have her brother's annoying accent. He raked his brain. What the hell was a water circuit?

"Restroom's by the escalators." Unsure if that was what she wanted, he led the way. "Follow me."

As soon as she disappeared in the restrooms, he exhaled and struggled to compose himself. He expected a more complicated encounter with a traditional, timid, scared woman. This confident, abrupt, beautiful girl unnerved him.

Scrubbing her face over the sink, Yasmeen felt cold water dampen the front of her dress. She examined her tired eyes in the mirror and noticed her white brassiere showing behind the soaked spots. She pressed paper towels against her chest. Did not work. She turned her blue scarf around and draped it over the see-through material. This was not a good start.

Fixing her hair, she reflected on her impression of the man outside. He seemed healthy and strong but walked with a slight limp. His hand did not work right. It was like shaking hands with a puppet, cold and loose. How could Fadi think this man could provide protection?

His attempt at speaking Arabic showed consideration. His smile reached his eyes, a good indication of an honest man according to her mother. And those eyes—what color were they? Gray? Green?

With one last look in the mirror, she decided it was time to face her husband again and walked out.

Slipping into the passenger seat of Adam's car, she held her purse in her lap like an old woman on a public bus and watched him in the side mirror place her suitcase in the trunk. He moved with ease given his damaged leg and hand.

Adam slid behind the wheel and turned on the engine.

"Buckle your belt, please."

Belt? Seatbelt. Right, they use these in America. She jerked the strap by her shoulder. The metal clasp refused to move. Twisting her body, she fumbled with the belt again, but the cursed thing seemed stuck. She let go and sat back. He must think she was an ignorant fool.

"It does not work," she huffed.

"Here." Adam extended his arm and pulled the

belt across her chest to the buckle. He smelled of soap and cedar wood.

"Gets stuck sometimes." A hint of amusement colored his voice.

Did he make fun of her? And why was he staring at her chest like that? How rude could he be? She hugged her purse tight and fixed her eyes straight ahead.

"Looks good on you."

"Excuse me?"

"My necktie. It's caught under your seatbelt."

Easing her grip on her purse, she tugged the tie out as fast as she could, feeling it slither between her breasts. Flustered, she offered it to Adam in a bundle.

He flung it over his shoulder to the back seat. "That's why I avoid wearing ties whenever I can. One can never know where they may end up."

She pressed her lips tight. If he meant to make a joke, she did not find it funny. There were far too many things she needed to know about this man, his sense of humor did not top the list.

Once they cleared the busy airport streets, they traveled on a wide speedway without going through the city of Chicago. The roads must have bypassed it. What a disappointment. She hoped to have a sense of the big city she saw from the air.

Adam pointed out scenery on the way but seemed to run out of words to describe flat land divided by one farm after the next. Some painted white, some plain, and some barely standing, wood fences zigzagged their way through open fields. How different everything looked, spacious and empty. What was the color of this side of earth? Everywhere her eyes landed, she saw greenery, grass, crops and trees. Gray asphalt provided the main contrast on the ground. Did people here plant every centimeter? Were there no empty patches to see the true composition of this land?

Father once told her people's temperaments followed the nature of the land they lived on. Bedouins were rough, their manners dry because of the harsh desert circumstances. Merchants were flexible due to their exposure to different places. Mountain people were tough and sturdy, dependable like the solid rocks under their feet. What did Father say about farmers?

She snuck a peek at Adam's profile. Small lines spread from the corner of his eye through the top of his cheek. He seemed too young to have old-age lines. Was that because he squinted under the sun while he worked his land? Making his skin glow the way it did? Did he laugh a lot? There were no bracket lines on the side of his mouth. Kindhearted and genuine, were the words her father used to describe farmers. Everything stayed on the surface, no hidden layers, he had explained. Merciful God, let Father be right.

Adam reached for the radio.

She broke her silence. "How far is your place?"

"It's a long way. Usually takes close to four hours."

Adam shifted in his seat, adjusting his left leg in the cramped space. "If you need to take a nap, I won't be offended."

"What is it?"

He raised his eyebrows. "Sorry?"

"What is nap?"

He cleared his throat. "I meant if you need to sleep, go ahead. You've had a very long flight. You must be exhausted."

"Oh! I am fine."

"Hungry?"

"No. Thank you."

"Many rest areas on the way. You say the word and I'll stop."

Although she had a good meal on the plane, her stomach churned at the thought of food. Maybe her apprehension and nervousness caused her body to burn more energy than needed. She waited for him to ask her again if she wanted to eat, but he didn't.

Back home, it was customary to reject an offer like that a couple of times before accepting. People were expected to insist, repeating the invitation. But she was not home, was she?

"What kind of plants do you grow on your farm?"

"It's a dairy farm. Most of the farms around here are dairy farms. We don't grow plants, we raise and milk cows."

"You do not . . . what is the word? Slaughter the cows to sell their meat?"

"We only sell fresh organic milk. The market's good and demand increases every year."

"Organic? What does that mean?"

"Produced without using antibiotics, hormones or pesticides." He glanced at her. "You know what those are?"

"Poisons to kill germs and bad insects." He really did think she was an ignorant fool.

"We raise our cows in open fields. Feed them grass. No animal by-products in their food."

"I have not seen a lot of cows at home, mostly sheep and they are raised naturally, I suppose. How can they be fed animal stuff and hormones? Would those products not show up in their milk?"

"Companies use them to speed growth and mass production. I don't." A smile softened his sharp features. "It's hard work, but we carved out a place in the market."

The seatbelt dug between her breasts. She crossed her legs, using the movement as a cover to adjust the belt higher over her chest.

"Is your farm as big as those we are passing?"

"It's actually one of the smallest in number of cows. One hundred and six to be exact." He pointed outside his window. "Those are industrial farms owned by large corporations. More than 600 cows. They use machines to milk them. I have several hired hands."

She detected a touch of pride in his voice. Tired and unable to relax, she placed her purse next to her feet and leaned her head back on the headrest.

"So, tell me about yourself." She might as well get the hard part out of the way.

"What do you want to know?"

"Were you ever in prison?"

"Never. Did you think your brother'd choose a criminal to be your husband?"

"Fadi did not have time to discuss things. Will it bother you if I ask more questions?"

"Not at all. I want us to get to know each other. So, shoot."

"Shoot what?"

"Sorry. I meant ask your questions."

"How old are you?"

"Twenty-eight."

"Were you married before?" She hoped he didn't catch the hesitation in her voice. "For real, I mean?"

"Nope."

"Neither have I. In case you were wondering."

He glanced at her.

Was that a puzzled look on his face? Better make things clear in case he thought she was divorced or widowed. He might expect certain things from her if he thought that. Maybe she should not try to read between the lines. Flipping down the visor, she pretended to check the scarf on her chest in the mirror, stealing a moment to compose herself.

"Do you have a big family?" She pushed the visor back.

"My mother passed away three years ago. No siblings. I live alone."

"My condolences." Did she sound too dry? Uncaring? Trying to clarify she was not heartless, she softened her tone, "You must miss her."

He gave a quick nod. "I do."

"Siblings," she slowly sounded the word. "Does that mean brothers and sisters?"

"Yup. Sorry about that."

"Do not apologize. I like to learn new words. What about your father?"

He took in a deep breath and released a gradual exhale. When he took too long to answer, she pressed on, "Is he dead too?"

"My father is dead to *me*."

Adam regretted his words as soon as he uttered them. His razor-sharp voice, his emphasis on the last word and the lack of emotion in his statement should have been enough to raise red flags in Yasmeen's face. Did she catch that? She didn't give him a sign. He let his sentence hang in the air between them for a few heartbeats, giving her time to dig into the topic of his father. She didn't. Smart girl.

Needing a diversion, he asked, "What did you study in college?"

"Visual Arts."

"You're an artist?" The enthusiasm in his voice a little exaggerated, but he hoped to lift the mood.

"I am not an artist."

At last, a full-blown smile was thrown his way, a bright sunny kind of smile. He took his eyes off the road longer than was safe.

"I studied art," she continued. "Its history and how different forms of art affected human development through the centuries."

"You must have talent."

"I wouldn't call it talent. I sketch using pencils and charcoal. A hobby more than a talent, really." Yasmeen was staring at her lap. He couldn't tell if she was being modest or embarrassed.

"Is there anything I should know about your person that is relevant to our . . . arrangement?" Her voice subdued, she sounded reluctant.

He checked the rear-view mirror and switched to the right lane, taking a moment before he answered.

"Never been in trouble with the law, if you don't count traffic tickets. Lived and worked on my family farm since I was a child. Served five years in the army. Never went to college." He chanced a glimpse at her. She hadn't moved.

"Who took care of the farm while you were away?"

"My mother with the help of hired hands. The Abeldeens are like family."

She remained quiet.

"Let's see. I don't smoke. Don't drink. I enjoy a—"

"Did you say you do not drink? How is that possible?"

Holding back a laugh, he cleared his throat.

"Alcohol. I don't drink alcohol."

Her cheeks turned bright red. "Oh, I see," she mumbled. "You need to speak plainly, I am afraid. My English is not that good."

"Way better than I expected. How'd you manage that?"

"We start learning English or French in secondary school. I learned more on my own from books, though. I love books. Plays. Poetry." She waved her hand in the air. "Anything I can get my hands on."

He took heart, finding one thing in common lightened the load on his shoulders. "I enjoy a good book when I'm not working. Have a decent collection at home."

"What else do you do?"

"Fix broken things, no matter how long it takes. You could call me a little obsessive. I can cook a good meal. Proud of a few recipes my mother taught me." Grinning, he tilted his head in her direction, trying to put her mind at ease. "I must sound boring to you."

"That is not important."

He sank lower in his seat. What the hell was that supposed to mean? Did she think he was boring or not?

"Do you have . . ." she swallowed, then dropped

her voice to a whisper, "outside the normal preferences?"

He gripped the steering wheel at the proper ten-to-two position as if it was his first time behind it. Where did she come up with these questions? He slowed the car to a stop on the shoulder.

Blushing, she dropped her gaze to her lap.

"I'm just a regular kind of guy." He softened his tone. "No surprises, I promise."

"I want to explain something. This temporary arrangement is not a marriage in my view." Her blush deepened. "It does not give you rights." She raised her eyes. "Do you understand?"

"Completely. Didn't expect otherwise. You have nothing to worry about, believe me. I know what kind of arrangement this is. Circumstances pushed you to it. I gave Fadi my word you wouldn't be forced into anything that isn't okay with you, and I always keep my promises. At least I try to."

He felt like a babbling fool. Why was he taken off guard by her request? He expected the topic to be brought up when the time was right. But the way she went about it threw him off.

"Really, no need to worry about . . . about that." Did he sound too assuring? What the hell was he supposed to say now?

"So, we understand each other."

Yasmeen averted her face to the side, but not before he caught her rolling her eyes. Great! Shethought he was boring and a blubbering moron.

CHAPTER 4

AN ARRANGEMENT

The steady glide of the car on smooth roads, and the absence of car horns that distinguish busy city streets lulled Yasmeen's senses. She drifted off to sleep. The car jolted her to reality, and she shielded her eyes with her hand to block the orange orb dominating the horizon. The day neared its end when Adam's car turned onto a dirt driveway off the main road.

Her stomach gurgled. She pressed the other hand to it, praying the sound wasn't loud enough for Adam to hear. Around this time back home, Mother would have prepared a big plate of fruits and called everyone to come together around the fountain. Several neighbors would have drifted in as well. Laughter rang throughout the house, dominating all noises, when life was normal. When life was at it should be. Where were Mother and Father now? Were they safe? What did they eat today?

Adam took another turn. Despite her discomfort, she was able to read a road sign indicating

"Shipman Farm" in black letters.

"This is it."

Confused, she craned her neck to read the sign again. "This is your farm? But it says Shipman on the sign, not Wegener."

"Shipman's my father's name. The farm belonged to his family. Wegener's my mother's family name. I like it better." It was obvious from his tone he didn't want to explain further.

Her pulse quickened. What kind of man discarded his father's name, and considered him dead while still living? Could such a man be trusted? Did Fadi know that about him? She turned her attention to her surroundings searching for markers in case she needed to plan an escape.

Pine trees lined the long driveway on both sides and ended at a paved square leading to the house. An odd-shaped pond with a mess of flowery plants centered the square. The non-circular pond looked like a teardrop to Yasmeen. She was about to comment about it but refrained when Adam stopped the car and asked her politely to step out.

The two-story house was painted a drab shade of gray. Her artistic eye rejected the offensive color. Why would anyone want to live in a gray house? To the left, stood a one-story rectangular structure, gray, with a single window and a huge two-paneled door facing the square. There was no clutter around, old tools or pots thrown aside. Everything was in place but looked depressing. The air smelled clean, even familiar. Was that jasmine growing next to the porch?

Adam carried her luggage up the three steps to the porch. He held the screen door open with his back and swung open the front door.

"Welcome to your new home."

The words hit her like a rock. Home? This was not home. She took a couple of deep breaths to steady her nerves and went up the steps. Paying attention to Adam's intimidating height, she squeezed past him, careful not to brush against his chest. She stopped a few feet inside. To her left, a huge living room with a fireplace, hard wood floors, multicolor rug and customary furniture. A staircase with wood railing led to the second floor. Unlike the exterior, the walls were painted bright white. Her spirits lifted.

He placed her bag on the floor and motioned to the right. She followed him into a bright kitchen furnished with white cabinets. The only color came from soft green drapes over a pair of windows and a matching tablecloth. The white countertops were bare, not a cooking pot nor a sugar bowl, or even a kitchen towel.

She turned and was struck by Adam's transformation. He had his hands in his pockets, a strange look on his face. Why did he stare at her like that? Was he nervous or something? Could he be waiting for a compliment? Did men care about things like that?

"The interior of your house is beautiful."

"Thanks. You're the first woman in here since my mother passed away. It's nice to hear." His face was somber, unsmiling. "Like to see upstairs?"

They moved together through the living room. The white walls lacked picture frames, paintings or artwork. Except for a single frame over the mantel, which contained a typed document.

A strange feeling played with her empty stomach. After his statement in the kitchen about his mother, she had no right to be privy to any of this. How come he did not have women in his house since she passed away? Did he not have friends, neighbors? What else was wrong with this man?

The stairs led to a short hallway connecting three bedrooms and a bathroom. Adam opened one door to the right and placed her bag on the floor. He flipped the light switch.

"This one will be yours. The guest room. We never used it."

Yasmeen entered the room. Walls were painted

a light shade of lavender, a queen-sized iron bed dressed in purple, and a matching curtain over the window. A painting depicting a field of sunflowers hung above the headboard. Two yellow towels were neatly folded and placed on an armchair.

Behind her, Adam's voice was gentle. "Is this okay with you?"

"Yes." She tried to hide her growing anxiety. Did she sound ungrateful?

"It is lovely." She added a hesitant smile.

"My room's right across." He walked over and switched on the lights in the opposite room.

She crossed the hall after him. The room declared masculinity in every aspect, beige walls, heavy wooden bed covered by a brown blanket, a similarly built desk and bookcase, a leather brown chair, and an ivory curtain. No paintings on the walls, no picture frames either.

"Help yourself to any of the books. They're sorted alphabetically." He led the way to the end of the hallway. "Bathroom's here." Stopping in front of a third room, he opened the door, but didn't turn on the light. "This was my mother's room."

Remaining beside him at the door, she peered into the darkened room and made out a bed in the center, two nightstands, and a chest at the foot of the bed.

"Mom died in her sleep." Adam brought his voice down. "You superstitious? This doesn't bother you, does it?" His face showed genuine concern.

She eyed the man by her side, seeing him in a different way. "The dead do not bother me. Only the living."

"It's going to be alright. I know this is difficult for you. It'll get better. You can trust me."

Yasmeen wished she could dissolve into nothingness. She should not even be here. How could living here with this stranger be safer than being back home with her family? Something churned inside her chest, like her mother's pressure cooker, about to eject steam and whistle the need for release. She backed to the hallway looking for an escape before she lost control. Her stomach announced its void with an audible growl and added embarrassment to the mix of emotions she suffered.

"Dinner will be ready in thirty minutes." Adam closed his mother's bedroom door. "See you downstairs?"

She nodded, hurried to her assigned room, and hid behind the door. Lowering her body on the bed, she clasped her cold and damp hands, her knees knocking against each other. Panic washed over her like a waterfall, one wave of violent sobs after the next. She clamped her hands over her mouth to muffle an immanent scream. She would not have *him* hear her cry, imagine her week, breakable.

An incessant phone ring from downstairs hammered her ears. The unanswered call accentuated the emptiness around her. Hugging her knees, she rocked her body back and forth. Minutes went by until spilled tears gave her relief.

The suitcase on the floor beckoned her to unpack. The process of putting away her clothes and few belongings subdued her. When she took out her sketchpad and charcoal pencils, her hands shook. Fadi had given them to her the day she left, told her to record only beautiful things from then on. Clutching the pencils to her chest, she bowed her head and burst into uncontrollable cries again.

Sounds of clattering plates drifted from downstairs and roused her to action. She tucked her precious collection in the nightstand drawer, grabbed a yellow towel, washed, and headed downstairs. She would live in this house, make it her home for the next couple of months, pretend she belonged, and then go back home to Damascus.

CHAPTER 5

AN AWAKENING

Adam's luck had run out. He dragged his feet through the desert sand, his sweat-drenched camouflage uniform weighing him down. He labored for breath, the air humid and full of death smells, rancid stench of decaying human flesh under the blistering sun. Above his head, a hawk soared. One, two, three enemy soldiers chased after him, their assault rifles at the ready. He could handle one or two, but for the third one, he needed luck.

A desert wind whirled around the three soldiers, halting their charge toward him. He breathed in sand mixed with sweat and sought cover behind a waist-high sand dune. The nearest soldier took aim.

Adam reached into his pocket and pulled out his knife, the only weapon he had left. He sent it winging through the air, it pierced the soldier's chest. The body vanished into the sky, taking the knife with it.

The second soldier glanced around in confusion. Adam bellowed, lunged at him, landing on his prone body, face to face. The soldier thrashed and screamed for mercy. Adam thrust a hand at the soldier's neck, circled it and squeezed, his other hand gripped the soldier's wrist. He held him trapped in an ironclad hold, afraid he would vanish like the other.

The soldier shrank under his grip, frail and powerless. When the soldier screamed again, it was not a battle cry, but an unusual soft sound. Adam couldn't understand the words. He loosened his grip.

"Open your eyes . . . Please. It's me. Yasmeen. Oh God! Wake up."

Strong kicks struck his rigid body again and again, and then a heavy blow to his groin.

He shrieked in pain.

"The soldier," he mumbled, eyes now open. "What— what happened to the soldier?"

"Dream. Get . . . off . . . me."

Her pale face jolted him like lightning. Shit. He jumped from the bed in horror, backing to the farthest wall. Heavy breathing and labored coughing were the only sounds in the room.

Yasmeen struggled to sit up in bed, her chest starved for oxygen. She looked at Adam in the dim light coming from the hallway. He trembled from head to toe, seeming at a complete loss. In the three weeks she had been here, this was the first time she saw him go through a night like this. "You were screaming." Violent coughs interrupted her words. "I shook you to wake you." She tried to stand but dropped back and sat on the edge of the bed. She clutched her throat and a series of coughs seized her.

"Drink water," he urged, backing further into a corner.

She took a sip from a glass on the nightstand and spit it out with another cough.

Shoulders hunched, hands balled into fists, he stepped forward. "You need help. I'll take you to Doctor Johnson's."

She attempted to get on her feet, plopped down again, still fighting to stabilize her breathing. "I'm—I'm . . . fine."

He turned toward the door, put his hands on the jambs, and hung his head. "Stay in bed. I'll bring Doc here."

"Turn around."

Seconds went by and he didn't move. "God help me, I choked you. Almost killed you."

"Look at me, please."

He dropped his arms to his sides.

She rose from the bed and went around to face him. The muscles on the sides of his jaw pumped. She touched his shoulder.

"Look at me. I am alright."

He flashed a tormented look.

"You were having a nightmare. It is over now." She swallowed hard. "I do not need a doctor. I am going back to bed and you should too."

Retreating into her room, she closed the door leaving him in the hallway. She extended her arms in front of her to feel her way to the bed, not daring to turn on the light. Just a regular kind of guy? No surprises, he had told her. God have mercy, he almost killed her. Connecting with her blanket, she hurried to slip under it and pulled it over her head. So he was one of those? Who fought with demons in their sleep?

After Fadi returned from Iraq, he had a couple of nights like these. But she only heard him suffer through them, never saw him. Father calmed him down, brought him back to reality, and stayed by his side all night. Adam had no one. He seemed lost, a savage look on his face when he first woke up, confusion giving way to fear. The horror radiated off of his entire body. How scared he must have been, to realize what he was doing to her.

She touched her neck, skin raw and throbbing. She needed to take something for the pain. Better wait until he went to sleep before she ventured out to the bathroom. *If* he ever went to sleep tonight.

How could he? Fadi used to talk the rest of the night with Father, their voices drifted to her room, and in a strange way, comforted her. It gave her a sense that everything went back to normal. It was too quiet, now. Adam had no one to talk to. Should she offer? What if he had not composed himself yet? And what would she say?

Lifting one corner of the blanket, she peeked at the light seeping in from under her door, the dark shadow of his feet clear. He was still there. Why would he not go into his room? She squeezed her eyes shut. Dear merciful God, have him go away.

Adam stood in front of Yasmeen's closed door, silent as a tree, hands still shaking. He listened to sounds from behind the door, coughing, or crying, or a movement to indicate Yasmeen was not alright. A minute went by, his ability to think disappeared with every ticking second. He knocked on her door, unable to bring himself to open it.

"Yasmeen, you sure you're okay? Let me look at your wrist, it probably needs some ice."

"I am really fine. Don't worry. Go back to bed."

He hesitated, conflicted, trying to decide if he should trust his instincts and go for the doctor. The hospital was out of the question. At least Doc knew him and his family. He wouldn't ask too many questions. Disgusted with himself for subjecting her to this side of him, he wished he could turn back the clock. He glanced at his watch, nearly three a.m. The drive into town would take twenty minutes and the old doctor would answer the door in his pajamas. What would he tell him? *I almost choked the life out of my wife in my sleep, so please come and check on her?*

He leaned his forehead against the door. "May I come in? I want to make sure you're okay. Your neck needs to be massaged."

"I already did. It is fine," a tremor in her voice. "I want to go to sleep now. I will see you in the morning."

***

The sun took too long to rise for Adam. He had spent the dark hours on the kitchen chair, drinking strong coffee, afraid to go upstairs or close to his bed. When Yasmeen walked in, he jumped to his feet and stepped back, keeping as much distance as possible.

She wore a white scarf around her neck. He looked her over, searching for signs of his attack. Did she think hiding her injury would fool him? He knew his own strength.

Approaching, her hands clenched together at the

front of her body. "Good morning."

God help him, she looked scared. He turned around and spoke to the kitchen sink. "Morning. Would you like something to eat?" His voice steady, controlled. "Before we go see the doctor?"

"I smell coffee." Yasmeen pulled out a chair, scraping the floor. "I would like a cup, please. And I do not need to go to the doctor."

He filled a cup and put it on the table in front of her.

Folding her arms on her chest, she took a step back.

He returned to his spot by the sink. She was terrified, not just scared. He didn't blame her.

Trying not to move her neck, Yasmeen lowered her body onto the chair. "You had a nightmare. I had my share of nightmares. Nothing too bad happened last night. You woke up in time and I am all right. A little bruised, that is all."

He leaned his body back onto the counter, lowered his head, and talked to the floor. "Do you know why your brother sent you to me?"

"Because you owe him your life and he asked for payback."

"Two of us were wounded and trapped in a house in Iraq. We both owe him our lives, but he chose me to protect you."

"We have gone through this before."

"Do you know why?"

"He told me I would be safe with you and I trust him, but I have no idea why you in particular."

"It's because I'm the best at what I do."

"You are the best at killing people with your bare hands?"

He snapped his head up. "That's right. Don't tell me you're fine. I know what I did. What could've happened a second too late?" He held the edge of the counter behind him. "You're more than bruised and we both know it." Pushing away, he opened the back door. "I'm taking you to the doctor if I have to carry you there."

She closed the distance between them and stood on the threshold. "Other than your promise to protect me, you promised my brother you would not ask me to do anything I do not want to do." Lifting her chin, she stressed her words, "I do not want to go."

"You need medical attention."

"The doctor will tell me to take pain killers for the pain and swelling. You have some in the medicine cabinet, and I took a couple. I will prepare my grandmother's herbal cream to help with the bruising." She averted her eyes to the side. "It will take a few days for them to fade. I am fine with that.

The doctor will try to find out what happened." Shrugging, she returned her gaze to his. "It is silly really, I am fine. If I feel that I need to go to the doctor, I will let you know."

He looked her over, from her scarf covered neck down to her wrists, concealed by long sleeves. He concentrated on the small birthmark on the back of her right hand. It matched the almond shape of her eyes with the outer corners lifted upward. Its color dark chocolate like her large irises, as if God intended her to have a third eye. Was she shaking? Struggling to hide her fear? Why? Why was she this accepting of what happened? He dragged his eyes to her face again, unsure if he should push the issue. Determination showed on her face. She had won. He would not force her to go.

"Promise?"

"I promise."

Just as he was about to step back inside, Yasmeen extended her arm to block his way.

"Would you like to talk about your dream?"

"I was in combat. Nothing to talk about."

CHAPTER 6

COOKIE

They prepared breakfast together. Yasmeen could not help becoming nervous by Adam's silence. He avoided any possible chance of getting close, concentrated on what he did, and looked anywhere but at her. The phone rang. He lifted the handset off the wall-mounted base, put it to his ear for a few seconds, and slammed it back. He did not say a word.

She thought it odd, even rude, but did not ask questions or interfere. During the meal, she chatted about everything she could think of to force him out of the strained silence. Frustrated, she ate her fried eggs in pain.

"I intend to take my morning walk."

"I'll be in the north field, just pass the barn. Close enough if you holler." Adam addressed the plate in front of him.

"What does that word mean?"

"Holler? Shout if you need anything."

Yasmeen's walk took her behind the house

toward a small lake and along the dirt trail following its shoreline. She marveled at the vastness of the open fields, a landscape she was not used to growing up in the crowded city of Damascus. Accustomed to being surrounded by many family members in her house, her most challenging issue since she arrived was the emptiness, and the loneliness it projected. Must she listen, and sometimes silence her mind's conversations in the long hours of the days? An art she had not perfected while growing up.

The trail ended at a huge maple tree, her favorite spot to sit under to reflect on her life, her journey to this foreign land and to a stranger for a husband. When Fadi told her he needed to send her away for safety reasons, she had not expected the process would trap her in a marriage as well.

Her strong brother had struggled to compose himself when he presented her with the marriage papers. Fadi did not look her in the eye, and she knew guilt kept him from doing that. He forced her to leave, and she preferred to stay, do her share in the uprising. He did not give her enough credit, thought of her as a burden.

In the end, she understood her brother's need to send her off, the urgency of his situation, and the lack of other solutions. So, she signed the cursed marriage contract and sealed her fate to a complete stranger. But she did not comprehend the tender emotions Fadi failed to conceal when he hugged her farewell, apologetic and awkward. It was like her brother said his final goodbyes to her that day. After all, she would go back in a couple of months when the madness was over, would she not?

At first, Adam's easy acceptance of the circumstances that brought her into his life subdued her. She began to feel hopeful. After what she experienced last night, her hopefulness crumbled into doubt.

The early fall wind picked up speed and combed the maple branches above her. Shouldering the curtain of falling red leaves, she felt the enormity of her commitment. What had she gotten herself into?

Back at the house, she busied herself with the usual morning chores. She prepared her mother's healing recipe, using lavender and mint leaves from the herb garden, and mixed them with flour and olive oil to make a paste. She rubbed the aromatic mixture on her neck and covered it with the scarf.

They ate lunch together, and she tried to hide her discomfort. Adam's eyes followed her every move. She started to clear the table, but he took over, suggesting she gets some rest. Yasmeen did not argue and went to her room, swallowed two pills for pain, and slipped into bed.

Opening her eyes to darkness, she rose disoriented and fatigued. It took her several minutes to get her bearings. She washed, brushed her tangled hair, readjusted her scarf and went downstairs.

Adam sat in the living room, reading a book, his hair wet from his usual evening shower. He regarded her with the same intensity of earlier in the day.

"How'd you feel?"

"Much better. Did you have anything to eat?"

"Made chicken noodle soup." He placed his book aside and rose from the chair. "Thought it might be easier for you to swallow. Let me get you some."

She followed him into the kitchen, taking a seat at the table. "A small bowl, please. I do not think I can have much."

While Adam had his back to her, she studied him, taking in details for the first time. Her eyes travelled over broad shoulders stretching the black fabric of his tee-shirt, muscular arms with skin that seemed to glow under the lights, down to long legs wrapped in faded denim. Would he get upset if she mentioned his slight limp? Or welcome the chance to explain it?

Last night was the first time she had any physical contact with Adam, or any man for that matter. As scary as it was, she tried to ignore this sudden interest in his sculptured body, an artful eye admiring beauty, nothing more. She searched for a distraction to talk about.

"Did you accomplish what you needed to do today?"

"For the most part. Still need few more days to secure the feed before the weather gets too cold."

"The feed?" Not familiar with the word, she seemed to be in constant learning mode when it came to his speech.

"Food for the cows."

"Is it going to get too cold for them, in the open like that? How do you keep them warm?"

"They spend winter in stalls." Adam turned to look at her. "Don't worry, I take good care of my herd. I've been doing this for a long time."

Yasmeen's cheeks warmed. "Sorry. I did not mean to suggest otherwise. I am trying to learn things, and the cows I have seen do not seem strong enough."

"Holstein cows don't look sturdy, but they're the world's best breeds for milk production. They're my livelihood." He returned to the stove. "It's my job to keep them in the best shape possible. Could show you the stalls, if you like. When you're better?"

"I would like that." She hoped she sounded enthusiastic enough. To change the subject, she asked, "Did you check the mail today?"

"Yup."

"Anything from my brother?"

"Nope."

The local newspaper lay on the table. Yasmeen flipped through it and scanned the headlines. Nothing in the small town interested her. She wanted to know what happened in Syria. Part of the agreement between her brother and Adam was to keep her away from news of home. For her protection, she was told. They did not know she needed protection from her own mind painting detailed images. Did they expect her to comply with this ridiculous rule? Once, she tried to watch news on the television while Adam worked outside the house, but there was no broadcast on any of the channels, just a white noisy screen.

"Why do you keep a broken television?"

"TV works fine. No antenna. Local channels don't get picked up. And I canceled my cable subscription."

"Why?"

"You know why. Fadi insisted on cutting you off about what's going on over there. At least for a while, until we hear from him." His hand hovered over the soup pot, holding a ladle. "And my laptop is password protected."

"You do everything Fadi says?"

The ladle clattered in the kitchen sink. "Don't know if it makes sense, but I made a promise, and I intend to keep it."

He brought over a bowl of soup. She folded the paper while he waited by her side. When he put the bowl down on the table, she noticed his hands, red with raw scratches. She reached out to touch them. He pulled them out of her reach.

"What happened to your hands?"

He sat across from her on the farthest side of the table and kept his hands in his lap out of her sight.

"It's nothing. Didn't wear gloves today."

"Why? They must hurt terribly."

"Forgot where I put the gloves yesterday."

"You should rub some antibacterial cream on them. Better yet, let me cut some Aloe Vera leaves to make a rub. I have seen the plant in your yard. It will soothe them." She pushed back her chair to rise, but Adam stopped her.

"Have your soup before it gets cold. I'll do it. I'll get the leaves myself and use them before I go to bed. Promise."

She could not argue with him since he used the same tactics she had last night. She worked on her soup with slight enthusiasm. Holding the spoon, her wrist ached, and her throat refused to cooperate.

The phone rang, cutting through the silence. She expected Adam to jump to his feet. But he sat like a statue, watching her. She concentrated on the soup and tried to ignore the beckoning call. The sixth ring got him off the table. His eyes remained on her.

"Don't call here again," Adam said the instant he put the handset to his ear and hung up. He returned to his seat. "If the phone rings, don't answer it." He offered no explanation.

Yasmeen nodded, reminding herself that the man had a life before she arrived at his doorstep. She must respect his privacy. When she deposited the bowl and spoon in the sink, she heard him move from the table. She turned around to find him at the back door, his jacket on.

"I'll be spending the night in the barn."

"Why?"

"One of the cows is ready to have her calf. Having difficulty. I need to be there."

"Which one is it?"

Despite his dark mood, Adam smiled. He

remembered how Yasmeen insisted on naming each cow she saw during the first days of her arrival. He didn't have the heart to tell her, sometimes, she named the same cow twice since she couldn't tell them apart. Now he struggled to remember the animal's designated name.

"Cookie," he ventured.

"You are spending the whole night? Where will you sleep in the barn?"

"There's a cot I've used before."

"But it is too cold. Surely you will need more than that jacket."

"It'll be fine. There's a heavy blanket in the barn. All you have to do is open your window and holler if you need me. I'll hear you. You'll be okay on your own?"

"Yes, of course."

"Night then. Make sure you lock the door behind me."

"There is no one around for kilometers. What if you needed to come in during the night?"

"Won't need to. Just do as I say please, it'll make me sleep better."

"Do not forget to rub Aloe Vera on your hands."

He waited until he heard her lock the door and headed to the barn. He wished he could hold on to her sweet smell while he checked on the barn animals, his ever-patient horse Earnest, the farm cats, and Cookie.

Stretching his exhausted body on the narrow cot, he looked up at her window, the light still on. He imagined her getting ready for bed, rubbing that aromatic herbal mixture over her creamy tan skin. He shifted his eyes to the moon, two days shy of turning full, filling the night sky with its usual silvery presence. Examining his hands in the moonlight, he rubbed them with the gooey juice oozing from the plant leaves. They ached but he welcomed the pain. All day, he went through the attack episode in his head over and over again, pushing harder with demanding labor, punishing his body for the harm it had done.

As much as his muscles wanted to surrender to a restful state, his mind resisted sleep. He tossed and turned, trying to get comfortable on the narrow cot. In the moonlit space around him, his mind took him to dark places and small closets. He went back to his childhood days, when he was five or six. Back to his room in this same house, where he would hide in his closet and wait for his father to calm down, stop yelling, stop punching, or just stop all together. He remembered what his mother's face looked like the next day, colored in places where make-up couldn't conceal anything no matter how much she applied.

His father became sweeter in the mornings, cooked them breakfast, made jokes, apologized for losing his temper the night before, and placed kisses on his mother's swollen cheek. Adam laughed at the jokes, felt happy if his mother managed a smile. He promised his mother to do his best not to grow up like his father.

Earnest neighed in his stall. Adam shifted his weight to flip on his back. He was fifteen years old then, on the morning of his birthday looking in the bathroom's full-length mirror, and feeling sick to his stomach. He saw a younger image of his father mocking his attempts to be different.

He walked his fingers over a scar five inches below his collar bone, evidence of the discipline sessions his father administered with a heated metal screwdriver over the years. The scar was physical evidence that he differed from the man who gave him his looks.

The light went off in Yasmeen's window. Adam closed his eyes and wished his head would stop conjuring memories. Memories of pulling his father off his mother for the last time one summer afternoon, a couple of months before he turned sixteen. Blinded by rage, he'd summoned everything he had to deliver his punches, too big for his closet, too big to hide. He had shoved his father in the car that same day and told him never to come back.

Inviting sleep to blanket his mind with anything but bitter memories, his father's voice echoed in his head.

"You think you're better than me, you little piece of shit? You're no different, you know. You're my son. Someday you'll see."

Seemed like his father was right.

CHAPTER 7

A LIGHT

Morning came sooner than Adam's fatigued body felt like it should. He had a sleepless night, his mind stuck in the past. It didn't help that the cats jumped around his bed, excited for the company, and Earnest objected with loud stomps and neighs, as if jealous for being left out of the party.

He washed using the hose out back and returned to the barn, rolling down his shirtsleeves, water dripping from his head.

Yasmeen stood by his cot, his work gloves in her hands. "I see you found them?" She sounded skeptical.

"Yup." He shouldn't have left them out for her see. He didn't expect her to come into the barn this early, either. Did she have a rough night too?

"Where is Cookie? Did she have her baby?"

"Not yet. Took her out to the field. Fresh air will help."

"You should have come in to wash."

"I managed. How're you feeling?"

"Better. Did you take care of your hands?"

He hid his hands in his pants pockets. "Didn't I promise I would?"

Yasmeen dropped the gloves back on the cot, frowning.

He kicked straw with the tips of his boots. "How about you? You didn't forget your promise to me, did you?"

"So far I am fine. I will make breakfast." She headed to the house.

Her skirt flowed from her tiny waist and danced around her smooth legs. Was she really as fine as she claimed?

***

On the morning of the third day, Yasmeen donned a brown sweater over jeans, wrapped a scarf around her neck and headed to the barn earlier than usual, determined to see Adam before he started work. Two days passed with the same rhythm. Adam worked until the sun went down and retired to the barn every night. Her bruises became more prominent as expected, and her discomfort in performing daily chores deepened. She was relieved Adam was not around to notice, but she suspected his absence was deliberate. It seemed odd the cow needed attending only at night. Meals were the only times they were together. Adam looked more exhausted and beaten, his hands not healing and his mood constantly dark.

Strong animal stench saturated her senses. Adam sat on the cot, both feet planted apart on the floor, his head bowed, arms rested on his knees. He looked tired. Tired and the day had not even started yet.

"Are you okay?"

He jumped to his feet and ran his fingers through his hair.

"You're up early today. Everything alright?"

"I need to talk to you before you get too busy."

He slipped past her to push the barn doors open. A breeze of fresh air came in, and she breathed a little easier. She looked around the barn in the early morning sunlight, searching for the cow again.

"Where is she?"

"Mind if we talk outside?"

She followed him into the open space and welcomed the move away from the barn's odors.

"Well? Where's Cookie?"

He nodded toward the distance. "In the pasture with her calf. She delivered last night. They're both fine."

"Does this mean you will come back to the

house tonight?"

Adam kept his gaze on the horizon ahead, shoved his hands in his pockets, and spoke to the top of her head.

"How do you feel today?"

"It is getting better."

"May I see?" His voice was almost a whisper.

She pushed up the sleeves of her blouse. Purplish fingermarks snaked around her right wrist. She expected him to take it in his hands to examine it, say something sympathetic. Instead, he nodded, then lifted his eyes to her neck.

Was he asking her to show him the bruise there? She fixed her gaze on his left shoulder, not expecting to feel uncomfortable, but it seemed so intimate. He had seen her neck before, so why the hesitation? But removing a piece of clothing to expose her skin was embarrassing. Back home, men did not ask women to do that, out in the open for everyone else to see. She looked around, feeling foolish. There was no one there but him, her husband.

"Please, Yasmeen." He towered over her, waiting.

She lifted her head to meet his eyes. The movement stretched her neck muscles, and she winced in pain.

"It's pretty bad, isn't it?"

To end this awkwardness, she unwrapped the scarf from around her neck.

Adam sucked a breath. The bruise covered most of her skin.

"I know it looks bad, but it does not hurt," Yasmeen explained, failing to convince him. "The herbal mixture is working well. It is drawing the crushed blood cells to the surface. That is why it has this deep color so soon."

He closed his eyes. His mother's discolored face popped in behind his eyelids. He pressed the base of his palms onto his eyes and dragged them down his face in frustration.

"I'm so sorry. I can protect you from any kind of danger, but I don't know how to protect you from . . . me." Disgusted with himself, he swallowed hard to stop a curse from escaping.

"Hiding yourself in the barn every night is not the answer. Cookie did not really need your help, did she?"

He remained silent.

"This is your home. I cannot forgive myself for driving you out of it."

"You're better off this way. Can't guarantee it won't happen again."

She held his red scratched hands. "Did you

mean to hurt me?"

He was helpless to move away, trapped by her touch, smell, voice, and dark brown eyes. She smelled of something earthy and inviting he couldn't name. The morning breeze chose that moment to play with the black silk of her hair. It danced around her gentle face. A strand twisted sideways across her cheek, teasing him. He had the urge to reach out and rub the hairs between his fingers. His hands remained prisoners of hers.

"No," was all he could say.

"Then stop punishing yourself for what happened. I am not as fragile as you think. I am used to violence around me. Do you forget where I am from? What my brother does? In the future, if you have another nightmare, I will leave you alone. In fact, I will not leave my room even if your eyes pop out." She patted his hands. "I will not let you hurt me again."

How many times had he heard his mother say those same words to his father? Little good did it do. He hurt her worse each time. Adam had to mentally shake his head to get back to this moment. He withdrew his hands and took several steps back.

"I am really fine." Yasmeen added a strange smile, hesitant and forced. Trying to put on a brave face, she seemed more vulnerable.

"There's a reason I live out here alone. There's a lot you don't know about me. What I'm capable of. I'm not . . . always . . . good company."

"You honored your word to my brother and took me in without knowing anything about me. Where I come from, a man's word is his worth. You opened your home and offered to share your life. Even if it is for a short time, I know I have caused an interruption to your plans, yet you do not ask for anything in return. You are an honorable man. That is enough to know."

He had never been called honorable in his life. The words forced their way through his defenses. Honorable man. How little she knew.

CHAPTER 8

A SAIL

Fall retreated fast. Adam insisted Yasmeen push her daily walks until after lunch to soak up some warmth. She got into the habit of taking her sketchpad and pencils, explaining her desire to capture images of her surroundings, snapshots to take back home. He offered his camera, but she declined. He expected her to show him her work at some point. She didn't offer. He didn't ask.

They danced around each other in the evenings when he retired to the house. He let Yasmeen set the pace and kept his distance. They spent most evenings with him lounging in his favorite chair with a book, and she on the couch working on her sketches. She borrowed books from his collection, and he noticed she went through them one by one in order starting with the letter A. She flipped through the Dictionary often or asked him the meaning of certain words. Some evenings, they watched movies, *Casablanca, The Godfather, True Grit,* and other classics from his DVD collection.

Yasmeen talked about her family. He listened and tried not to reveal any of the information Fadi had told him. She talked about her mother and father at home taking care of family matters when life was normal. She didn't seem to know her father was captured, or what her brother's fate might be after his return to Syria, or what happened to her mother. At times he talked about his mother, and Yasmeen listened with polite interest.

Comfortable with the new rhythm, for the first time in his life he didn't dread the bleak winter months. That thought triggered a concern about her winter gear.

"We need to go into town tomorrow."

Yasmeen lifted her head from the sketchpad in her hands. "I thought it was best for me not to be seen by many people."

"For your protection. But you need winter clothes and unless you trust my taste, you need to go with me."

"I have enough, I do not need anything." She returned to her pad.

"I thought women liked to shop." He didn't know any who refused the chance. "Besides, you don't have what's needed for a Wisconsin winter."

Yasmeen remained occupied with her sketch. "What would you say to those who ask about me?"

He set aside his book and studied her from his chair, curled up with a blanket on her lap, her hand moving fast over the paper. He called her name. She looked up with a smile.

"You're my wife. I'll tell them that." He challenged her to say something contrary.

She held his stare. Shadows of the flames in the fireplace danced on her serious face. "So why have you asked Mr. Abeldeen and his son to stay away from the house?"

If she meant to surprise him, she failed. He knew everything that happened on his farm. "Ben told me he ran into you yesterday by the lake. You failed to mention it." He meant to sound as authoritative as possible. She should have told him.

"Did I break a rule or something?" Yasmeen pressed on. "If you are trying to keep my presence a secret, why would you take me into town and expose me to people there?"

"Expose you?" He leaned forward in his chair, clasped his hands between his knees for lack of something to crush. "First of all, I'm not keeping your presence a secret. I told the Abeldeens to stay away for a while because I wasn't sure how you'd handle two more strange men around." He tried to keep his voice calm. "If you haven't noticed, you weren't entirely accepting of me."

She opened her mouth to say something, but he cut her off. "Second, I myself don't go into town if it isn't necessary." He softened his tone. "Thought I'd give you time to adjust to life here before you had to deal with other people."

She closed her sketchpad and set it on the coffee table. "It is very lonely here. I am not used to being alone so much. My father is the oldest in a family of twelve siblings." She raised her eyebrows and flattened her lips, as if expecting him to admire her use of the word.

Keeping his face straight, he hid his amusement.

"It is a cultural tradition to assign our house as the center for every family activity."

"Haven't thought of it that way." Of course, he wasn't enough company for a young woman like Yasmeen.

"If it was not a celebration for a religious event, a cousin's birth, a graduation or an engagement, our house was a place to hold funerals, solve family disputes and spend evenings just for the sake of being together." She stretched her legs on the couch, adjusted the blanket over her knees. "I have twenty-six cousins. Someone was always around."

"Amy, my friend Jonathan's girlfriend, is waiting to meet you. You'll like her."

"Are you not concerned about what your friends

will say after I leave? I mean do they know about me? How and why I am here?"

"Jonathan's the only one who knows the circumstances of our marriage. I trust him with my life. Amy doesn't know specifics."

"You do not think Jonathan told her?"

"No. Not her. Not anybody else."

"You cannot keep these things a secret for too long."

"Didn't go into details with anyone about anything. The less known about you the better, for your—"

"Protection. Yes, I understand."

He exhaled a long breath. "I'm trying my best."

"You could also try walking with me some afternoons. Would you mind?"

"I'd like that."

***

Yasmeen half-listened to Adam's description of Mrs. Merick's role in the small town, fretting about encounters with strangers, uncomfortable, apprehensive and worried all at once. Thanks to Mrs. Merick, the small town had an upscale boutique, offering women an opportunity to purchase the latest fashions.

Yasmeen sat beside Adam in the car, hair tied in a ponytail. She wore a pair of jeans, her pink turtleneck and one of Adam's thick jackets he had insisted she should put on. The day was cold yet sunny, and it became warmer inside the car. Adam's jacket introduced smells and triggered emotions foreign to her. The freshness of shaving cream, the spice of a man's cologne, the warmth enveloping her as if Adam had his arms around her.

She should not have agreed to come. What was wrong with wearing the same pair of jeans every day? She might need a jacket, but she could get used to wearing his for the short stay. What would people think of Adam, the way she was dressed today? Drowning in his big khaki jacket? He had been so kind, so respectful. He deserved to be seen in a good light.

Tightening her hold on her purse, she avoided looking in Adam's direction and remained quiet, listening to music on the radio.

Adam parked the car in front of Blooms Boutique on Main Street. He turned to her. "Ready?"

She grabbed her purse, got out of the car, and walked into the shop ahead of him while he held the door open. A small bell above the door announced their entry.

"Heavens! Is that you, Adam?" A woman squeaked from the other end of the shop.

"Hello, Maryanne." He moved in front of Yasmeen, blocking her view of the woman.

Yasmeen stepped to the side to see.

Maryanne maneuvered around decorated racks of elegant clothes to the front. She wore a short black dress exposing long legs and black knee-high boots. A huge silver anchor rested on top of her bosom, pointing to a generous cleavage. She looked like she was in her late thirties.

Maryanne wrapped her arms around Adam's neck. "Am I dreaming?"

He winced, placed his hands on her shoulders, and waited for the hug to be over.

Yasmeen stood by watching, counted multiple rings on Maryanne's long fingers, and admired straight blond hair. The intimate behavior astonished her, a show of emotion like that between a man and a woman in public. Perhaps Maryanne was his aunt? No, Adam would have told her. And the woman seemed but a few years older than him. There were many customs she needed to learn here. Even her own reactions were strange to her. She acknowledged the funny feeling in her stomach and blamed her nervousness.

Maryanne pulled back. "Dear me, I didn't see

you there, honey." She extended hands jingling with multiple bracelets.

Adam's voice came flat. "This is my wife, Yasmeen."

Maryanne's hands reversed their progress towards an embrace and flew to her chest. "Your wife?" The statement clearly surprised the woman.

Yasmeen smiled, looking to Adam for guidance. He placed a hand on her shoulder. "Meet Mrs. Merick, a dear friend of mine."

Maryanne's recovery was painful to witness. She darted her eyes between Adam and Yasmeen, her hands twisting the cross on its chain. She then snatched Yasmeen's left hand. "I don't see a ring, Adam. Is this a joke?"

"This is not a joke, Mrs. Merick." Yasmeen tried to keep her voice kind, but firm at the same time. She retrieved her hand, glancing at Adam. His face dropped. He seemed embarrassed and lost for an explanation. "I assure you we are married. I did not want to wear my ring while I shopped. It might catch on some thread and ruin a garment."

"Garment?" Maryanne repeated. "Where is she from?" She addressed Adam. "Is she a foreign student or something?"

"Yasmeen needs winter clothes. Thought your shop the perfect place to begin." He moved toward one of the racks, dragging Yasmeen by the hand.

She glanced behind to see Maryanne's eyes follow them, pursing red painted lips, disbelief written over her face. Yasmeen felt like a child being taken care of by an adult, helpless to prevent the woman's obvious undoing.

Adam's hold on her hand was firm and welcomed. The simple act satisfied a flittering sensation spreading inside her chest, another foreign feeling triggered by seeing Adam in this woman's arms. She turned her attention to him when he tugged the jacket off her shoulders and held a heavy coat for her to try.

Maryanne overcame her shock and the sales talent within prevailed. She approached them, listing the coat's superb qualities.

"You must excuse me, my dear," Maryanne, at last, addressed her. "I was totally taken by surprise." She shot Adam a look that spoke volumes. "You've come to the right place."

Adam retreated to a corner, leaned against the wall and watched Yasmeen consider the merchandise. Her eyes checked back with him every now and then. He noticed the gradual change in Maryanne's attitude toward her and attributed it to Yasmeen's calming demeanor. She chatted with

Maryanne as if they were longtime friends, discussing fabric patterns and styles, things he had no idea about. Yasmeen's favorite color was purple. She shied away from busy patterns, preferred cotton to wool, didn't care for shades of gray. She picked out practical clothes instead of fancy ones and refused high heels.

Yasmeen would disappear in the fitting room, then come out with the new items in her hand, back on the hangers. If only she would model the outfits, especially the red one, ask his opinion or something. In the end, he resigned to being an observer.

Yasmeen excused herself, saying she needed to talk to her husband. She asked him to follow her to the back of the store away from Maryanne's ears. Blushing, she seemed hesitant.

"What's wrong?"

"There is something you need to know." She spoke in a hushed voice, looking at her feet rather than his face.

"What?" He could tell she was embarrassed and hoped it wouldn't be about some feminine thing he was unaware of. He bent his head closer. "Just tell me."

"I cannot afford a single item here," Yasmeen whispered.

"I can." He snapped his head back. "Did you

think I'd ask you to pay for anything? What kind of man you think I am?"

"Please do not feel insulted." She placed her hand on his bare forearm. "Can you at least tell me your budget, before I get too involved?"

Her simple contact went beyond his skin, triggering a deeper sensation within. She was showing signs of concern for him. Was this intentional? Or had he been that deprived of female company, he read too much in an innocent touch? Shit. He cleared his throat. "Just pick what you want. My pockets are deep."

She frowned, withdrawing her hand.

"That means my budget's big enough. Don't worry about money."

Yasmeen ended her shopping spree, gave Maryanne a tight hug, and accompanied Adam to the diner across the street for lunch, stopping to deposit multiple bags in his car. Heads turned toward them in the diner. They sat in a booth by the window.

"Everyone noses in everyone's business in a small town like ours. Don't be surprised if other people behave like Maryanne. The worst is over. You handled her well."

The collar of his plaid shirt curled upward when

he took his jacket off. She caught herself reaching over to fix it and grasped the saltshaker instead.

"*You* could have handled her with a little more care yourself."

"Maryanne? What do you mean?" Adam ran his hand over the back of his neck and fixed his collar.

She twirled around the saltshaker in her hands. "The woman had her heart broken, and you used me to do it."

Adam sat back as if her words slapped him. "Why'd you think that?"

"I may be innocent in your eyes, but I am not naive. I know how the world works. Maryanne Merick is obviously more than a dear friend to you." She bit her lower lip. Stupid girl. She should have kept her mouth shut. What did she know about matters like these? Nothing.

A young waitress with a bouncing ponytail placed menus on their table, winked at Adam as if Yasmeen were invisible. "Hey, Adam. Haven't seen you in a long time."

"Give us a minute, Gloria."

"Sure, just let me know when you're ready." Gloria walked away.

"Seems your opinion of me keeps finding lower levels. Are you suggesting I have something deeper than friendship with a married woman?"

She tried to dig her way out of the hole she put herself into. "I am not suggesting. I have no intention passing judgment, either. I just do not want to be the cause of anyone's misery."

"Maryanne's misery has nothing to do with you. She's a true friend. Visited Mother all the time while she was sick. She may have feelings for me … right. But I never encouraged her or took advantage of her. I do have principles."

She read something on his face. Honesty? Did American men not brag about such affairs? What was she doing? She knew nothing, nothing about American men, or men in general. "I can understand why she would have feelings for you. You are a good man. You could have made the news of our marriage easier for the poor woman, that is all," she softened her tone. "The way you did it was cruel."

Adam's exhale was long and deep. "Bought half her store. She'll get over it. Trust me. I'm not the first man she set her hopes on and didn't get anywhere with. Sometimes, we inflict misery on others no matter how hard we try not to."

"I suppose you are right." She leaned forward in her seat. "It has been a very difficult morning for me. Maryanne was critical and judgmental. She asked a lot of questions, but I tried to keep her busy by discussing her merchandise. It was obvious she was unhappy. Where is Mr. Merick, anyway?"

He removed the saltshaker from her hands and placed it back where it belonged at the end of the table. "Alive and well. He's the mayor."

She studied his solemn face, realizing his obsession for order was a force she needed to pay more attention to. Did her talk about Maryanne make him angry? Did she cross a red line? How could she smooth things between them?

"Thank you for all the clothes. You have been very generous. I do not think I will need them when I go back home. Maryanne said we could return what I do not wear and get your money back. I did not tell her I was leaving, of course. But I asked, just in case."

A muscle under his left eye twitched.

Did she make it worse? She did flatter him, did she not? Pointed out his generosity?

He signaled at Gloria, who was cleaning a nearby table, and indicated they were ready to order. "We need to make another stop before we head home. Let's have lunch." He buried his face behind the menu.

"But I don't need anything else."

"You need a wedding ring."

CHAPTER 9

AN ISLAND

Keeping his promise, Adam accompanied Yasmeen on one of her afternoon walks a couple of days later. They ended up hitching a ride with Ben Abeldeen to escape the swift turn of the weather. Ben had spotted them while inspecting the fence before the storm hit full force.

On the bed of Ben's beat-up truck, Adam trapped Yasmeen on his lap. Her warm body pressed against his, sapping his control. With two of the Abeldeen children in the passenger seat, and the truck bed full of farm essentials, Adam pushed aside a couple of tools and climbed in the back, leaving Yasmeen no room but to curve her body in with his. And she fit, nicely. He could have sat sideways, pulled his legs together so she wouldn't have to be caged between them, but he didn't.

He sensed her uneasiness, holding his bent knees while the truck traveled the bumpy road. Stiffening her body to avoid more contact, she only stoked his fire in the process, her attempts making her more desirable. Her hair played with his nerves in the wind, and he caught a good whiff of her flowery scent.

Once they arrived home, he waited to use the bathroom after Yasmeen finished getting ready for the night. Her inviting smell hung in the air and hit him full force. Alone in his bed, sleep eluded him. Her scent was all over him, as if she lay beside him sharing his pillow.

Every cell in his body yearned for a touch, Yasmeen's touch. Every thought in his head disintegrated into a carnal image. Every moment spent away from her, forced a greater need.

He stared at the ceiling wide-awake, anger replacing mounting frustration. Why had he let her come so close tonight? He was doing fine, comfortable with the system they had fallen into. Why did he stretch his limits?

His blanket crumpled at the foot of the bed, the cotton sheet covering his naked body turned the bed into an oven with the creeping hours of the night. Giving up on sleep, he kicked the sheet off, slipped into pajama pants and a tee-shirt and headed for the kitchen. He needed to take his mind off the woman across the hall. Perhaps he could satisfy another animalistic urge as a means for fulfillment.

The cold air from the open fridge eased a

modicum of his discomfort. He stared at the open fridge longer than needed before he collected ingredients of a sandwich. Keeping the kitchen lights off, he used the fridge light to spread a generous amount of mayonnaise on a piece of toast. He piled on cold turkey cuts and topped them with a slice of cheese and lettuce.

Satisfied by the good-sized sandwich on his plate, he closed the fridge and ate standing by the window, watching nature's fury unfold outside, feeling like a teenager more than a grown man. What was going on with him? He managed to keep women out of his life so far without having to suffer through nights like these. Why did he have this strong pull toward Yasmeen? Why now? She was a woman counting down the days until she left. She never even uttered his name. Not once did he hear her say it. Was it a cultural thing? Women didn't call their husbands by their first names in her part of the world? Not likely. It was her, reserved, disregarding this marriage, keeping him at a distance, even in her mind. Why couldn't he do the same, damn it?

Yasmeen entered the kitchen, opened the fridge door and grabbed the milk pitcher. Silhouetted by the light, she wore a white night robe cinched tightly at her waist. She was barefoot.

"You couldn't sleep either?"

Yasmeen swung around. The milk pitcher in her hand struck the fridge door handle and broke, spilling milk down her robe and scattering glass shards.

"Don't move!" He sprinted forward holding up his hand. The look on her face froze him a couple of steps away. Eyes wide, face as white as the spilled milk, jaw shut tight. "So sorry. Didn't mean to startle you."

Yasmeen raised her hand with a sharp piece of the glass pitcher and pointed it at him. "Do not come any closer!" Her voice shook.

"Yasmeen, it's me, Adam." He lowered his hands. "Please don't move. There's broken glass everywhere. I'm going to switch on the lights."

She waved the broken glass like a dagger and screamed. "Stay away from me."

Keeping his distance, he inched toward the light switch.

Her hand moved with him. "Do not come near me."

Adam flipped the light switch. "Dear God!" He choked, absorbing the sight in front of him. The right side of her robe was bright red. Blood ran down her legs and pooled at her bare feet. He looked for the source of the blood. The other end of the makeshift dagger was imbedded in her right wrist.

"You cut the artery in your wrist."

Her right hand shook, she steadied it with her other hand.

"I'm not going to hurt you." Heart thumping, he grabbed the hand with the glass dagger, lifted her off the floor, and headed to the back door.

Yasmeen made a feeble attempt to push off his chest, she whimpered, and her eyes glazed over. Shit. She's going to pass out. He shoved the injured arm above her head and tightened his fingers around it to slow the blood flow. So much blood. Hell, he'd seen enough blood in his life. Not her too. Not Yasmeen. "Stay with me. Don't close your eyes. Do you hear me?" He carried her like a rag doll out the back door, snatching his car keys off their hook. "I'm taking you to the doctor."

Running toward the car in front of the barn, freezing wind slapped at him. He leaned her limp body on the side of the car, yanked the passenger door open and swung her inside. He took off his tee-shirt and wrapped it as tight as he could above the bleeding gash, tied the other end of the shirt to the handle on top to keep her arm elevated.

Yasmeen's head slumped on her chest. He lifted it with his bloody hands and slapped her. "Don't sleep!" He yelled. "Open your eyes, damn it."

He fastened her seatbelt, slammed her door and ran to get behind the wheel.

He made it to town in twelve minutes, despite the sheets of heavy rain. He kept talking to Yasmeen, turned the heat to maximum to keep her warm.

Doctor Johnson lived in an apartment above a small clinic. Adam slammed on the brakes in front of the clinic and rammed his hand on the horn. The lights turned on. He carried Yasmeen out of the car and ran inside.

Without niceties, Doc instructed him to lay Yasmeen on a bed, opening drawers and pulling out medical supplies. She mumbled something in Arabic. He thought she was unconscious, bringing his head closer, he raised his voice. "I don't understand what you said. You're going to be alright."

Yasmeen opened her eyes, her voice barely audible. "Do not leave."

"I won't. I'm right here." He hoped she heard him before her eyes rolled back in her head, and she passed out.

Doc began working, shooting questions at the same time. "You know her blood type?"

He had no idea. "Don't know." He stood on the

other side of the bed, holding Yasmeen's cold left hand, rubbing it in his icy hands. It was pointless but he needed to do something.

Doc prepped a bag of blood. "Who is she, son?"

The words rolled with ease on Adam's tongue, "My wife."

Doc elbowed him out of his way. "I need to do an IV. You remember the drill."

He remembered, alright. Too many times he'd helped his mother to this very room and   watched Doc revive her.

Doc inserted a long needle in Yasmeen's arm. "Could she be pregnant?"

He shivered. "No."

"Pull that blanket from the bed behind you and try to warm up. Sit on the stool if you plan to stay in here. This will take some time."

Doc worked in silence. Either he needed it to concentrate, or he was considerate of Adam's physical and emotional state.

Adam welcomed the break. He wrapped himself with the blanket but didn't feel warmer. He sat on the stool by Yasmeen's head, placed his hands on either side and stroked her hair. His bloody handprint across her cheek pained his eyes.

Yasmeen's eyelids fluttered before staying open.

"You're in the clinic. Doc's working on your injured hand."

"Hold her arms still. Don't let her move them. I need to extract the glass."

Adam stood to get better leverage. The blanket fell off his shoulders.

Yasmeen's head lifted, panic on her face. "Do not leave."

He placed a hand on each arm to prevent her from moving. "It's okay. Just lie still so Doc can help you. I'm not going anywhere, sweetheart."

She put her head back, tears rolled down both sides.

"Can you give her something for the pain?" He wished he could free his hands to wipe her tears.

"Already gave her a sedative. She'll sleep soon." Doc squirted liquid over the wound.

As if on cue, Yasmeen's eyes closed. Her muscles relaxed under his hands. He dropped his tense body back on the stool and wiped her tears with his thumbs.

The doctor's wife, Rose walked in, slipping on gloves. "What do you want me to do, Frank?"

Rose was in charge of the clinic. The couple had known him from childhood, treated him for every mischief he fell into, and cared for his mother.

"Take care of him," her husband pointed with

his head.

Rose touched his shoulders. "Come with me, Adam. Let's wash the blood off and find you a shirt."

"I can't leave her." He looked through fog, not seeing anything but Yasmeen's red cheek.

"Let's just step to the sink over here and get you cleaned. You don't want to scare her when she wakes up, do you?" Rose led him by the hand to a sink in the corner and washed the caked blood off his chest and arms.

He kept his eyes on Yasmeen. "I'm supposed to protect her."

"Can you tell me what happened?" Doc's question penetrated the fogginess in his head.

"It was an accident." He recounted the event as best he could.

Doc listened, stitching the wound closed. When he was done, he lifted his head, switched off the spotlight, and shoved the surgical tray aside. He examined Yasmeen's body, checking for other injuries, Adam supposed. Good idea. Rose handed him one of the green shirts nurses wear in hospitals, and he slipped it on.

Doc worked in methodical steps, starting at her bloodied feet. When he reached her neck, he looked at Adam. "What happened here?"

He heard the accusation in the doctor's voice and didn't blame him for it. "It was an accident," he repeated. "I had a nightmare. She got caught up in the middle of it."

"This injury is at least ten days old. Why didn't you bring her to see me when it happened?"

"She wouldn't let me." Adam knew he disgusted the man. It showed clear on his face. He stepped closer. "Look, I know what this looks like. I swear to you, everything that happened to her was an accident. I never meant to hurt her."

"Rose, take over." Doc grabbed his arm and dragged him to the hallway. "I've heard this before, son. Same words, same defense. You know who I mean, don't you?"

He jerked his arm out of the man's grip. "Don't give me that crap, Doc. I'm not like my father. You know that."

"All I know is that I have a young woman in there, who you claim is your wife, with signs of battery and an attempted suicide." Doc's voice hardened by the second. "You tell me what to *give* to you."

Adam couldn't believe his ears. Attempted suicide? Shit!

"What the hell are you saying? I told you what happened."

"I urged you long ago to have an outlet for your violent tendencies. Haven't you learned anything from the life you had as a child?" Doc maintained a cold stare. "I hoped not to see you follow in your father's footsteps."

"I didn't hurt my wife, Doc. How can you think I did? You know how I tried to help my mother. I made a promise to myself long ago, I would never do that to a woman. You've got to believe me."

"I want to, Adam. But I'm afraid the odds are against you."

"What odds? I am my own man."

"You should've had professional help, son. I have a duty to find out what exactly happened."

He didn't want to have this conversation. He didn't want to be in the hallway. "People can change their destiny, Doc. You told me that yourself, remember? Why don't you ask her what happened when she wakes up?" He went back into the room. "Right now, I need to be by my wife's side."

Rose was washing the blood off Yasmeen's legs. She had cleaned her face. Hurrying closer, he helped remove the bloodied robe. The metallic scent of blood mingled with the sour smell of spoiled milk. Yasmeen would want to be rid of it. Rose tucked a warm blanket around Yasmeen. He stroked her clean cheek with the back of his fingers. "She's so cold."

Doc fiddled with the stand the IV bags hung from. He replaced an empty blood bag with a full one. "She lost a lot of blood."

"When will she wake up?"

CHAPTER 10

A REVELATION

Adam held Yasmeen's bandaged right arm, trying to prevent her from doing damage to the wound. "Take it easy, Yasmeen."

Yasmeen struggled to get off the bed and begged to go home. Rose pushed her back and checked the IV in her arm. Doc stood by the door, retreated there after Yasmeen screamed not to touch her when she first woke.

"Do not leave me here. Please take me home. Please!"

"Use the restraints, Rose," Doc instructed from the door. "We can't have her exerting her body like that. You need to calm down, young lady. We're here to help you."

Rose pulled a pair of padded leather cuffs from a drawer. She fumbled with one to put it around Yasmeen's left hand.

Yasmeen snatched her arm away, kicked her legs and twisted her body. *"La'a, ma biddi, ma biddi*. I do not want you to do that!" She screamed, her eyes wide with panic.

"Back off," Adam commanded.

Rose froze.

He bent over Yasmeen and looked into her hysterical eyes. "I'm taking you home."

She stopped thrashing, sweat dampened the hair around her face and mingled with her tears. She reached up with both arms and held on to his neck.

He held her in his arms, rocked her and patted her back. Crying, her body trembled, and he felt the tremors run through him. He used tender words to sooth her. Words flowed with ease through his lips, words he never uttered before. She finally calmed down.

"I want to take instructions from the doctor on how to care for you at home. I'm not leaving. Don't try to get up." He eased her head back onto the bed, smoothed damp hair off her face. "Be back in a minute."

Yasmeen closed her eyes and nodded her head. He motioned to Rose to join him by the doctor's side.

"You can't take her home yet." Doc shook his head. "I need to talk to her. In private."

Adam ran his hands a couple of times over his face. "You've seen how upset she is. She's scared."

Doc gave him a suspicious look. "I'm aware of that."

Adam raised his eyebrows. "You think she's afraid of me?" He leaned his face closer. "You can't keep her against her will. She wants to go home, and that's what's going to happen." He pulled back. "You and Rose can come with us, if you like. Set her up in the house. You can ask her all the questions you want, once she's settled."

"It's obvious my presence is agitating her." Doc sounded hesitant. "Rose, call Nurse Clive and see if she's available to look after Mrs. Wegener."

"I'll go, Frank," Rose interjected. "The sun is almost up, and I need Nurse Clive here in the clinic. We're giving flu shots, remember?" She placed her hand on her husband's arm. "Adam has a point. She'll feel safer in her own bed. I'll monitor the IV and stay with her for the rest of the day. I was planning on taking the day off, anyway."

"I still want to talk to her first," Doc insisted. "Find a way, Adam. Go tell her that."

Clenching his jaw, Adam went back to Yasmeen's side, touched her hand.

She opened her eyes. "Can we go now?"

"Soon. Doc needs to ask you few questions. It's important."

"I do not want to talk to him."

"Don't be afraid." He sat on the edge of the bed. "Doc has to hear the details of what happened from you, that's all."

"Then we can go?"

"Yes. Can I tell him to come in?"

"Wait. Where is my robe?" She pulled the blanket up to her chin.

"Rose had to get rid of it. It was very bloody. You're decent enough, Yasmeen. Don't worry." Taking a guess at the source of her hesitation. "Ready?"

"Yes." She sounded unsure.

He got off the bed and waved for Doc to come closer, Rose following behind. Yasmeen clutched the blanket on her chest, curling her uninjured hand into a fist. Adam gently rubbed his fingers on the back of her fist to relax it.

"How are you feeling now, young lady?"

"Tired."

"Do you remember what happened? How you injured yourself?"

"The milk pitcher broke in my hand when I was startled."

"So, it was an accident?"

"Of course. I thought there was an intruder."

"What about that old bruise on your neck. Can you tell me what caused it?"

Adam withdrew his hand. He took a couple of steps back. "Any papers I need to sign before we leave, Doc?"

Rose pointed toward the door. "Front desk."

"I'll be right back, sweetheart."

On his way out of the room, he heard Doc say, "Don't be afraid. I can help you. Just tell me what happened."

Walking down the short hallway to the front desk, Adam knew there were no papers ready for him. The doctor had to finalize his report first. As for payment, the bill should arrive in his mailbox in a couple of days.

He sat on one of the plastic chairs by the wall, massaged his aching leg, rested his head back and closed his eyes. He could hear their voices but couldn't understand what was being said. It was better this way. Let Doc get the facts for once, the old hypocrite. He knew exactly what his father did to his mother, and he never did anything to stop it. The concern he showed Yasmeen did not fool Adam one bit. He resented the coward doctor for not helping his mother as much as he despised his father for beating the crap out of her, breaking her piece by piece, inside and out. Doc thought Adam was like his father, had the audacity to judge him. What the hell did he know about his character? Not a damn thing.

Doc appeared at the door and called him back. Adam walked into the room. Yasmeen was on her feet, supported by Rose. He closed the distance and scooped her into his arms.

She rested her head on his shoulder. "Take me home now."

Yasmeen slept in the back seat of the car all the way, her head on Rose's lap. Adam drove into the breaking dawn, careful not to jerk the car, looking out for broken branches and mud puddles left by the storm. Good thing, bringing Rose with them. She would see the damage in the kitchen herself and put the issue to rest. How would he explain the sleeping arrangements? Maybe he could sneak his clothes to Yasmeen's room behind Rose's back. No, that would be silly. He didn't need to answer to anyone, damn it. It was his house. Let her make her assumptions. The Johnsons made up their minds about him long time ago.

He glanced in the rear-view mirror. Rose's eyes were closed, her head leaning on the window. He couldn't see Yasmeen. Why was she so afraid in the clinic? Terrified by the doctor?

They reached the house just as dawn gave way to the rising sun. He carried Yasmeen in.

Rose followed, carrying a box with medical

supplies. She went to work arranging things for her patient, instructing Adam to pull the curtains together, asking him to bring extra pillows and a fresh nightgown.

He opened Yasmeen's closet and found a white short-sleeve gown with ruffles decorating the neckline. Holding it out, he turned to Rose, who was fussing over sleeping Yasmeen. "Will this do?"

"Fine. Give me a hand." She removed the clinic blanket off Yasmeen and pulled the dirty gown up her legs.

It was like someone punched him in the gut. This was wrong. He was *not* going to undress her in her sleep, for heaven's sake.

"Don't just stand there. Help me lift her so I can slip this off."

"Cut it off. The gown's ruined anyway. She'll never want to wear it again." He turned his back and placed the clean gown at the foot of the bed. "I need to check on my men. See if they took care of things this morning. I was supposed to have the early shift. Be back as soon as I can." He headed to his room, changed into work clothes and went outside, breathing a little easier.

An hour later, he returned to the house to find Yasmeen tucked in her bed.

Rose sat on the chair with a book in her hand, a knotted trash bag by her feet. She stood as soon as he came into the room. "I'd like to prepare something for her to eat when she wakes. Can you stay with her while I do that?"

"Sure. The kitchen's a big mess. Haven't had the chance to clean it."

"I'm sure I can manage. You should be by her side when she comes to."

He wished he could take a shower first. He smelled of sweat and dried blood before he went to see the Abeldeens, and now the odor of heifers and bulls clung to his clothes.

Yasmeen opened her eyes. "What time is it?"

"Almost nine. How do you feel?"

She tried to rise. "Dizzy."

"Let me help you." He went to her side and placed a couple of pillows behind her back. He drew the curtains aside, letting the morning light in.

"Where is the lady?"

"Downstairs, fixing you something to eat. You hungry?"

"A little, but I am afraid I might throw up." She rested her head back, studying him in the bright light filling the room. "You must be exhausted. I am sorry I put you through this."

He leaned on the windowsill, stretched his legs

forward, and folded his arms. Healthy color started to return to her face, big brown eyes becoming less ghostly.

"If anyone needs to apologize, it's me. I shouldn't have scared you like that. Wasn't thinking straight last night. Really sorry."

Yasmeen sank lower in bed. "We are even then." She went quiet for a minute. "The doctor thought I tried to kill myself. He questioned me when you left the room." She twisted the edge of the comforter on her chest with her fingers. "He said he had known you since you were a boy. Why would he say something like that?"

"My mother attempted suicide twice. I was the one who intervened both times." He tried his best not to let the pain filter through his voice, hoped she would stop her probing.

Yasmeen narrowed her eyes, and he knew she would press on. Just knew it. Damn it.

"How old were you?"

"Does that make a difference?"

"If it is too difficult for you to talk about, then never mind."

"I was nine the first time. Mom took sleeping pills and lay down for an afternoon nap. I couldn't wake her for dinner. Doc had to pump her stomach." Keeping his voice flat, he suspected he sounded like he was reciting a story. "The second time, she tried to drown herself in the lake. I was fifteen, big enough to pull her out. She never learned to swim." He took two steps closer to the bed. "Want to know why she tried to kill herself?"

"I know why. Your father was mean to her."

He balled his fists by his sides. "Fred beat the life out of her. I wouldn't call that being mean. He was more than mean. He was an animal."

Yasmeen turned her head toward the window and fell silent, seeming lost in thought.

He flexed his fists and berated himself for adding the emotional load to her current state. Why did she have to ask? And why, in God's name, didn't he keep his mouth shut?

"I have seen men behave worse than animals. When I first woke up, I thought the doctor was one of them."

CHAPTER 11

INHALE

Yasmeen's words echoed in Adam's mind. Stunned, motionless, he waited for her to say more, or clarify what she meant. He cleared his throat. Mute and unresponsive, Yasmeen's face remained turned toward the window.

Rose's footsteps on the stairs silenced him. She walked into the room with a tray in her hands and proceeded to serve Yasmeen. Rose chatted and chattered, but he had no idea what she said. Taking the trash bag, he excused himself.

He spent several minutes cleaning the kitchen floor. Rose had done most of the work. He recounted Yasmeen's last statement while he worked, trying to conjure up scenarios she might have witnessed rather than experienced, hoping he misunderstood all together.

On his way to take a shower, he passed by her room, door open. Rose sat on the bed, her back to the door conversing with Yasmeen in hushed tones. He connected eyes with Yasmeen. Her lips broke with a hint of a smile, shy and tentative.

His steps faltered, and then he continued, summoning unattainable wishes. Yasmeen could be his real bride, lounging in bed without a care in the world. He could be the one who prepared her breakfast. The old woman could be his mother, alive and happy with her daughter-in-law.

Stepping into the steaming shower, he washed the self-pity away.

***

Adam walked into Jonathan's shop. Flat on his back, Jonathan cursed from under a muddy car, its model and color undistinguishable. He dragged himself out and grabbed a screwdriver from a toolbox by his feet.

Adam hovered over his head. "Hey."

Jonathan squinted. "Hey, man. You look like shit."

"I feel like shit."

Jonathan jumped to his feet, grabbed a rag and wiped his grime-blackened hands. He stood four inches shorter than Adam, with the same athletic build, but a good twenty pounds heavier.

"If marriage does that to a man, I'll stay single," Jonathan's voice boomed.

"Good luck finding a woman who'd marry

you," he shot back. "Can this heap wait?"

"Sure." Jonathan tossed the rag over his shoulder. "Is this serious?"

Clenching his jaw, Adam headed to the little room in the back that served as storage space and office.

"Yup, serious enough, I see." Jonathan followed, poured a cup of coffee, and tried to hand it to Adam.

"When was the last time you washed this mug?"

"What's today? Wednesday? It's clean enough, freak." Jonathan removed a Styrofoam cup from a plastic bag next to the coffee machine, filled it, and offered it to Adam. "What's weighin' you down? Honeymoon over?"

Adam sat on the only chair in the room, behind a workbench. He looked at his smirking friend. "Honeymoon never started."

"What, you couldn't . . . perform?" Jonathan chuckled the last word and slapped his thigh. His out-of-place laugh died when Adam shot him a disgusted glare.

"What the hell, man. What did you do?"

"I hurt her."

"God damn it! How?" All humor disappeared from Jonathan's voice.

"You want to know about the first time, or the

second?"

"Fuck. Talk to me."

The weight of his actions pressed down on him. Feeling like Atlas, he struggled to keep his shoulders straight. "The first time, I strangled her in my sleep."

Jonathan sprayed coffee in his direction. "Holy shit!"

"Then I accidentally made her cut her wrist and almost bleed to death."

"What the fuck!"

"If you pick up a book every now and then, you might be able to add other words to your vocabulary."

"All that self learnin' didn't do you any good. At least I never attacked my gal."

He jumped to his feet and shoved Jonathan against the wall. Coffee spilled on the floor, boxes tumbled down from overstuffed shelves.

"Take it easy, man. I'm only kiddin'."

Giving Jonathan a gentler shove, his anger deflated, and he backed off. "This *is* serious. Can't think straight anymore. Don't know what to do. Every time I come close to her, I end up making a bigger mess." He returned to the chair. "It's like I'm on a mission to destroy her, not protect her."

Jonathan sat on the edge of the bench. "Why

don't you explain things to me? The Adam I know can never hurt a woman. What happened?"

He looked at Jonathan's hand, the grime under his fingernails too prominent to ignore. He didn't know where to start.

"Where's your wife now?"

"Home with Doc's wife. I needed to get out of there before I did something stupid. Can't stay for long."

"How does the old hag fit into this?"

"Rose came home with us last night after I took Yasmeen to the clinic. Yasmeen refused to stay but still needed medical attention. Rose volunteered. That was the best I could come up with."

"That bad, huh?"

"You have no idea." In short terms, he told Jonathan what happened.

Jonathan paced the small office space. "Told you this was a mistake. No man in his right mind marries a foreigner the way you did. Have you even thought about the law in this?"

"What do you mean?"

"I checked with my cousin, Sam. You know, the attorney in Milwaukee? Unofficially, of course. He said you have ninety days from the date of entry to apply to change her status from spousal visa to residency, did you know that? It's been almost two months already."

"She thinks she'll go back soon. How can I convince her to sign something like that when she's considering leaving?"

Jonathan scratched his head. "You mean you haven't won her over with your charmin' personality?"

"Very funny."

"Nothin' happened between you two? I mean other than the attempted murder and stuff, did you get—"

"I know what you mean," he interrupted. "Don't go there. This is my wife we're talking about. No joking matter."

Jonathan lifted his hand to his forehead in a mock salute. "Yes, Sir! You heard from her brother at all?"

"Nope. We agreed to communicate through Big Scott. He keeps checking for me. Fadi's back in Syria. Managed to stay undetected so far. His name hasn't appeared on any list Human Rights Watch issued, so most likely he's still alive. But three of her cousins are listed as missing. Haven't told her that. Don't think she knows about her father either."

Jonathan put both hands on the bench, leaned forward. "Maybe you should tell her."

"And scare her? There's nothing she can do."

"She has the right to know about her father, at least."

He ran a hand through his hair. "If Fadi wanted her to know, he would've told her himself."

"Put yourself in her shoes, wouldn't you want to know? Maybe she could say a prayer or somethin'."

He hadn't seen Yasmeen pray since she arrived. Muslims performed prayers five times a day, had seen it in Iraq. Fadi in particular was very prompt, yet she hadn't done that as far as he knew. Maybe she wasn't the religious type. Maybe she was hesitant to practice her religion around him. Maybe she'd lost her faith all together.

"Don't know any more," he said in frustration.

"Don't you think she has a good idea what's goin' on over there? She must suspect somethin'," Jonathan pressed.

"I've kept her in the dark so far, no news. That was the agreement. Fadi insisted. Thought he didn't want her exposed to what's taking place, but she said something this morning that . . . I don't know, man, it made me worry."

"What?"

"I think she was traumatized somehow. Oh, hell, I don't know. It's just the way she said it, the look on her face scared me."

"What did she say, man? Maybe you

misunderstood."

"She said she's seen men behave worse than animals, and thought the doctor was one of them. She was hysterical in the clinic, screamed at Doc not to touch her."

"What do you think she meant?"

"Don't know." He put his elbows on the bench, ran his hands over his face, and laced his fingers on top of his head. "Don't want to know."

"Why don't you ask her? She obviously wanted to talk about it."

Dropping his hands, he lifted his head. "You think so? I think she was overwhelmed after I told her about Mom's attempted suicide and Frank's abuse."

"You sure know how to make a woman feel safe. Why the hell did you do that?"

"She drew it out of me."

"It's time Amy and I visit you. Friday evenin'?"

"That's fine. Yasmeen's been lonely." He checked his watch. "Have to go."

Jonathan walked him out to his car. "I ran into Maryanne yesterday. She was really pissed. Said you spent your savings on that little immigrant wife of yours in her store." He held his palms up. "Her words, not mine."

"Actually, I spent most of my savings in Mr.

Polensky's store on a diamond ring."

"Yeah, I heard. Thanks a lot, man. Couldn't you have chosen somethin' modest?"

"I needed to make a point."

Jonathan slapped him on the back. "Maryanne finally got the message. So did every other woman in town accordin' to Amy." He shook his head. "Women!"

"I needed to make a point to Yasmeen."

"Yeah? How'd she take it?"

"She tried to choose something mediocre. Told her no wife of mine's going to walk around with anything but the best. She got the point, I think."

Jonathan nodded. "Now I'll never hear the end of it from Amy. She'll expect a big rock when I pop the question."

"Any time soon?"

"I'm in no hurry," Jonathan closed the car door."I'm not encouraged by your experience."

CHAPTER 12

EXHALE

The evening sky was clear. The early sunset added a sharp edge to the cold wind blowing in Adam's face. On his front porch, he waited while Doctor Johnson conferred with Rose about Yasmeen's condition. Doc decided not to go inside to avoid another frantic scene, so he waited in his car. Rose went in to fetch the unused medical supplies and say goodbye to Yasmeen.

Adam held the front door open for her when she returned. "Can't thank you enough. You've been very kind."

She laid a wrinkled hand on his arm. "Oh, hush. I was only doing my job. I'd like to visit with your wife once she's better, if that's all right with you."

"Of course." He wondered if she wanted to check if Yasmeen was still alive.

"Make sure she eats well and gets plenty of rest. I know you'll take good care of her, son. Interesting gal you've got there." Rose walked out and waved goodbye, before her husband drove off.

Despite the cold seeping into his bones, he postponed going inside as long as he could. The door to Yasmeen's room was open. He peeked in. She was awake.

"May I come in?"

"Yes." She sounded stronger and looked better than this morning.

Taking the chair, he stretched his aching leg in front of him. "You left quite an impression on Rose. She likes you."

"She talked too much. Rose has interesting features. I think I will do a sketch of her face."

"Talked about what?"

"Her daughters. You. Your mother."

He rested his elbows on the chair arms. "What I said earlier about my mother—"

"Is something private and I . . . app . . . apprehensive for the confidence you gave me," Yasmeen interrupted. "We all have our breaking points."

"Appreciate. The word is appreciate." He faked a cough to hide his amusement.

"Oh, thank you. I knew I said it wrong. The pills Rose gave me are making me drowsy." Yasmeen fiddled with the blanket. "Are you not interested in what Rose told me about you?"

"I don't care about her opinion of me." He

didn't try to keep his deep resentment of the Johnsons from surfacing.

"She did not give her opinion. Rose told me facts. Your mother was not the only one your father hurt." Her hands stopped twisting. "He used to hurt you too."

***

Yasmeen looked around in the dark and tried to focus on her surroundings. Her mouth was dry, her head pounded, her wrist throbbed with pain, and she was sweating from head to toe. The digital clock on the nightstand blinked 4:05 a.m. Adam would wake up soon. She needed a shower, clean clothes, to brush her hair. She turned on the nightstand lamp, took a couple of pain pills, and peeled the covers off. Her bare feet landed on the cold floor.

Shivers ran up her damp body and she wrapped herself with the comforter. Taking a deep breath, she pushed off the bed, steadying herself with the help of the footboard. When the floor under her feet stopped tilting, she headed to her closet, dug out a clean outfit, and tiptoed for the bathroom. She stopped in front of Adam's open door.

He was face down, spread-eagled on top of the covers, head turned toward the door. The light from her room revealed how haggard he looked, his beard making a comeback. His shirt twisted and gathered above his waist, revealing part of his back. Her eyes caught a mark on his side. She inched closer, the bottom part of a tattoo, round, black, and unclear. If only she could lift his shirt to figure out what it was.

Adam stirred and flipped his head to the other side, brought his arms up to hug the pillow, lifting his shirt a few centimeters. More of his tattoo showed, twisting curvy lines. Still unclear.

She shivered again, remembered his long embrace, the sweet words he whispered in her ears, telling her not to be afraid. Focusing on his voice broke her free from the horrid place her mind took her to last night in the clinic. A scary place thousands of kilometers away, a place she could not forget. If she told Adam why she was so terrified, would he understand? Would he still look at her with those light eyes of his in the same way, kind and reassuring? Would it matter if he did not? Being honest with oneself was a necessity, Father had taught her. *Lying to yourself served nothing but inviting others to lie to you.* She tightened the comforter around her shoulders. Yes, it would matter. A great deal.

Fadi was right. This stranger proved he could be

trusted. She should find a way to thank him when he woke up, show him some gratitude. Maybe coming here was a good idea, after all. Having to stay a bit longer would be fine too, if circumstances required it. Why had Fadi not called her yet, like he promised? Where were Mother and Father? What would they think of all of this, their daughter standing in her nightgown a couple of steps away from the bed of this foreigner? If only she could talk to her mother, hear her voice. What would Adam do if she picked up the phone and dialed home? Maybe one of her cousins would answer and tell her where her parents were. Should she ask for permission first? Would she jeopardize everything if she did not? Would she cause him to lose his trust in her?

Stepping back out of his room, she went into the bathroom, and shut the door as quietly as she could, trying plans in her head, weighing options, and failing to reach convincing answers.

Pain pills carried her through until sunrise. In the kitchen, she tried her hand at making a hearty breakfast when the pain in her wrist returned, insistent and unrelenting. Pushing her tolerance threshold, she tried to finish the omelets, but the spatula dropped from her hand and skidded across the tiled floor, causing a loud clatter. She sat at the table out of breath and energy, her hand shaking.

Stomping on the stairs signaled Adam's fervent approach. He called for her, a measure of panic in his tone. Before she could answer him, he barreled into the kitchen, looking like he had been thrown out of bed and down the stairs. The tails of his rumpled shirt hung out at odd angles outside his jeans, hair matted on one side of his head, and deep lines ran across his left cheek.

"What do you think you're doing?"

"Good morning to you too."

"You shouldn't be out of bed." He pulled his chair next to hers. "You scared the daylights out of me when I didn't find you there."

"I feel better. I made breakfast. Where would I go?"

"You should've woken me." He ran his hand over his hair, fixing nothing. "Your hair is wet. You showered? Didn't Rose say you shouldn't get the bandage wet?"

"Rose left me a plastic bag to cover the bandage with." She was not a child and she would not let him treat her like one. Why was he so angry?

"You must be as hungry as I am. Everything is ready, but would you please bring the plates to the table. I need to eat something so I can take my pills."

Adam moved fast, serving the spinach omelets

she prepared with toast. He placed a glass of water in front of her. "I'll get your pills."

Yasmeen put her hand on his before he could pull it away. "Let us eat first."

He gazed at their joined hands, seeming even angrier.

She snatched her hand back, feeling like a guilty child, not knowing what she had done to make him mad.

***

Adam lingered around the house all afternoon letting the Abeldeens take care of things for a while. He went over numbers in his books to make sure he increased their pay this month, keeping in mind he didn't have much of a cushion anymore, and still needed to pay Doc's bill.

Scanning his calendar, he noted the coming inspection for organic certification. The inspectors weren't scheduled for another two weeks. He had time to double check compliance before they arrived. Trusting Ben didn't stop him from going over details, making sure his farm passed inspection with flying colors. He took a quick peek at Yasmeen after she retired to her room to sleep the hours away.

Mrs. Abeldeen stopped by with a potato and chicken casserole and fresh baked bread. She asked about Yasmeen's health and left without disturbing her.

Yasmeen refused to be served in bed, and they had an early dinner in the kitchen. The late afternoon was calm and the temperature tolerable, unusual for this time of year. They moved to the front porch to drink hot tea.

Trying to stay discreet, he studied Yasmeen when she wasn't looking. She sat in one of the rocking chairs, wrapped in his mother's lap blanket, hair loose, legs crossed, a serene look on her face. Was it possible she'd started to accept being here, being with him? Disregarding everything that had happened? Not likely. She hadn't once uttered his name, remaining reserved. But she reached out to him in the clinic, and it felt right to have her in his arms like that. It felt right to have her by his side this evening.

The panic he experienced when he woke this morning and didn't find her in her room was irrational. She was right, where would she have gone? Yet he felt the spark of fear all the same. Fear of failing in his duties? Fear of being alone again, of losing Yasmeen in particular? He stretched his legs and crossed his ankles, relieving the pressure building up in his left leg. This was not the time to analyze his feelings. He needed to find out what scared her, what he had to deal with before he got too involved. If it wasn't too late.

"How do you feel now?"

Yasmeen turned toward him with a serious look. "I feel safe."

Like applying soothing balm on a burn for him, but too good to believe. Suspecting his face betrayed his skepticism, he searched for an opening to draw her out. "You don't have to be careful around me. You can talk to me."

"What would you like me to talk about?"

"Yesterday, when I told you about my father, you said something before Rose interrupted. I'd like to know what you meant by it."

Yasmeen looked away into the distance. She went quiet for a stretch of time, seeming lost in thought. Adam waited, hating to push her. Did he give her enough cause to trust him with her secrets? Not with the way he'd behaved so far, attacking her in his sleep and scaring her to death last night. Why would she confide in him?

"Do you know what an old traditional house in Damascus looks like?"

"I've seen traditional houses in Iraq with a roofless square in the middle and the rooms open to it."

"It is similar to that. Our house is a two-story, traditional home in a very old neighborhood, an original structure that has been in the family for generations. We had an inner courtyard with a fountain in the middle, an orange tree, an herb garden, rose bushes, and crawling jasmine just like the one you have here." She rose and approached the branches crawling up the side of the house. She looked back at him. "I can't believe it has not lost all its flowers yet. Can you help me reach those on top?"

He pulled a high branch and lowered it within her reach. "The barn blocks most of the cold wind. It'll go dormant when snow falls."

He used the branch as an excuse to get closer, pulling it further down, fearing it might snap any second. He didn't care. A gust of wind pushed Yasmeen's hair away from her face, revealing faint vertical line at the top of her forehead. A childhood scar, maybe? Should he ask? What was she like as a child? Quiet, dreamy, or defiant and difficult? He ran his thumb on the branch in his hand, wishing he could do the same to that scar.

Yasmeen plucked the delicate white flowers, collecting them in her palm. "Our bedrooms were upstairs and their windows opened to the courtyard, not to the outside." She seemed too occupied in her task to notice their closeness, her tone wistful. "I used to make flower necklaces and hang them on the orange tree branches. Jasmine perfume filled the house in the evenings." She buried her nose in her overflowing palm, closed her eyes, and inhaled deep.

Dreamy, she must have been a dreamy, happy child. Taking advantage of her distraction, he moved his hand down the branch. His knuckles almost brushed her cheek. The contrast of the white petals with her dark eyelashes captivated him.

"Mom loved it." He was breathless, as if he'd been running for miles. He tucked a flower behind her ear.

She dipped her head and turned sideways, giving him a clear view of the pulsing vein in her neck. His crazy mind started counting her heartbeats.

"Our neighbors in surrounding small apartment buildings envied us because our family held on to the house and did not tear it down to build something modern. My best friend, Z . . . Zainab, lived in an apartment building, and she loved to stay at our house. We spent most summer evenings around that fountain, no need for air conditioning." She curved her lips in a sad smile. "I always imagined my wedding would be in our courtyard by that fountain."

The branch escaped his hold, vibrated on the wall under her bedroom window. The leaves rustled and showered them with more fragrance. Losing the branch meant losing the excuse to keep his body close. He leaned his shoulder to the wall and pretended to examine the sturdiness of the twining branches.

"I had the only room in the house with an additional window. It was on the inner corner away from the street and opened to our neighbor's garden. They kept it full of flowers in the spring. Beautiful deep purple roses mostly."

"Your favorite color."

"How do you know that?"

He inched forward until he was sure she felt his breath on her face. "I pay attention." His mind lost count of her heartbeat, but he could swear the pulse in her neck quickened.

She stepped to the side and faced the open field.

"When I was little, I used to think I was very lucky to have this special room. Fadi took the room by the stairs toward the street, so his friends could come straight to his room when they visited without having to go through the rest of the house. And he had many visitors. Handsome, educated young men."

A black and white kitten strolled by and rubbed its body against Yasmeen's leg. She bent to scoop the fuzzy fur ball and brought it close to her cheek.

"Z . . . Zainab and I imagined ourselves in love with almost every one of them." She glanced at Adam. "Teenage girls, you know what I mean?"

He nodded. Why did she stammer every time she mentioned her friend's name? He didn't know where she was going with her story, how this memory trip could answer his question about what she meant when she mentioned seeing men behave worse than animals. But she was letting him into her life, and he welcomed that. He flexed his fingers, wanting his hand to be the one caressing Yasmeen's cheek instead of the cat's back. He cleared his throat. "You feel up for a walk?"

Yasmeen kissed the purring kitten's head and put her down. "I need my jacket." She turned to go back to the house.

He held her elbow. "I'll get it." He lingered his hand longer than necessary, his need to touch her too compelling. Dashing into the house, he snatched both their jackets from behind the back door and returned to her side as fast as he could manage, ignoring the stab of pain from his injured leg.

She dropped the collected flowers in her pocket.

They headed to her usual path, the kitten flounced around their heels.

"Anyone in particular catch your eye among Fadi's friends?"

"All of them." She broke in a shy smile, oblivious to his state of mind. "I used to sit outside Fadi's closed door and listen to their political discussions. I distinguished their voices, matched them to their names and faces when I saw them." Her smile vanished, and she stopped, fixing her gaze on a distant spot. "I wish I had not."

"Why?" He nudged her elbow to resume their walk.

"The summer I turned fifteen, our neighbors moved out of their house in the middle of the night, and armed men in plain clothes guarded their front door. My father said the secret police had taken residence there. *Mukhabarat.* He closed my window with wood planks. Until then, I crossed in front of that house every morning to meet Z . . . Zainab at the end of the street so we could walk to school together. My mother told me to keep my eyes down to my feet, never to look up at the guards' faces, to ignore anything they said to me. I even learned to distinguish their voices." She shivered.

He draped his arm around her shoulders. "You want to go back?"

Yasmeen shook her head. "Let us sit under the maple tree." She folded her arms over her chest and kept walking.

"Did those guards bother you?" He dreaded the information he was seeking.

"They did things to people." She slowed her pace, swallowed and seemed to be working words in her head.

He ran his hand up and down her shoulder. "What kind of things?"

They reached the maple tree. Yasmeen sat on the lowest branch and motioned for him to sit by her side. He lowered his body next to hers, extended his legs in front of him and crossed his ankles.

Yasmeen's gaze was fixed on the low sun. "I have not told anyone." She shook her head. "I could not."

The flower he'd tucked behind her ear fell to her shoulder. He plucked it off. "Can you tell me?"

"This is not an easy thing for me to talk about, but I owe you an explanation about what happened last night."

Hooking his index finger under her chin, he turned her to face him. "You don't owe me anything."

Her lower lip trembled. "You should know. I want to be fair to you."

Fair would be to let him kiss her, stop that trembling. Struck by the thought, he held his breath for a moment. What was he thinking? Not now. Not when she was trying to get something off her chest, trusting him with a secret. "What happened?"

She hung her head. "Fadi's friends stopped visiting, and he spent more time away from home, sometimes for several days at a time. Once, I woke up in the middle of the night to someone screaming. It came through my special window even though it was closed. At first, I thought someone in the neighbor's house was sick or injured. As the screams continued, I recognized the voice. One of Fadi's friends. Nabil, with the round glasses and smooth face. I also recognized another voice. It belonged to one of the guards."

Knowing the answer beforehand, he needed to ask anyway. "What did he say?"

"I could tell he was interrogating Nabil. I never heard a man scream like that before. I could imagine what he did to him. Sometimes I sketched it, but hated looking at it so much, I ripped the papers to pieces."

"You didn't tell anyone?"

Lifting her head, she looked defensive. "I thought of telling Father, but what could he have done? He was worried about my brother's political activities already. I did not want my mother to hear or know about something horrible like that. I could not ask Fadi to listen to his friend being tortured, so I told no one."

He gave a quick nod. At fifteen, she carried a cruel burden alone. He knew a thing or two about that himself. "I understand."

"Over the next ten years, almost all of Fadi's friends, some of my cousins and other men screamed through my special window. At quiet times, some men prayed for God to show His power, some cursed a lot, some cried. And some . . . sounded like they would die of pain. I think a few did." Her voice sank deeper. "One night, I heard a woman's voice." Drawing a long breath, she pressed a hand to her belly. "Oh! Her screams. It sounded like she was in labor."

His chest hurt. He realized he'd held his breath for too long. He exhaled.

"I remember when my youngest aunt delivered her first son. The woman screamed like her." Yasmeen's voice almost disappeared. "That night, I heard a baby's first cry. The woman did give birth, and the baby was alive."

Adam chewed the inside of his cheek until he tasted blood.

"I heard men laughing, followed by a loud

thud."

His arms and back muscles tensed with trepidation.

She ran her hands down her face, wiping tears. "The baby went silent. I imagine they hit him with something hard or smacked his head on the ground. The last thing I heard from the mother was a song, you know, a special one to help babies sleep?"

"A lullaby." Adam found his voice with difficulty.

"The mother sang it through the whole night, until she too was silenced. I never learned who she was. I kept waiting for the men to say her name, or her husband's, so I could tell him what happened to his wife and child."

"He's better off not knowing."

"At first, I did not know why they were interrogating everyone. Then I learned that Fadi was one of the targets they looked for, that he was one of the leaders of the underground opposition movement, like that woman's husband. *Mukhabarat* wanted to know my brother's identity. I heard Father argue with him once after he left us for a whole week. He told him to slow down and be careful." Grabbing the hem of her jacket, she twisted the fabric. "They knew what happened to people who got arrested, but no one talked about it, so I saw no need to provide details."

He rubbed her back and tried to steady his voice.

"Can't imagine how you endured it night after night."

"The scariest part was listening for screams, searching for my brother's voice when he disappeared on us like he did. And I still had to go to school every morning, cross in front of those guards, knowing what they did the night before. Sometimes, when they washed the yard, red water ran under the front gates to the street. I had to walk carefully to avoid stepping in water mixed with blood."

"I'm so sorry you had to go through that." Worthless words. What could he possibly say that would help? Nothing.

Yasmeen looked toward the fireball melting in the horizon. "It became normal life for me. The screams even stopped waking me up at night. Days went on. Fadi left for Iraq when it became too dangerous for him, I went to college, and my window stayed shut."

"People find ways to survive and cope. There's nothing to feel guilty about."

She put her head on his shoulder.

He embraced her, rested his cheek on top of her

head. Darkness would soon set in, and he didn't bring a flashlight. "Let's go back to the house before it gets too dark." He helped her up, kept her nestled in his arms, walking in silence.

When they arrived home, Yasmeen sat on the couch and draped a throw blanket on her lap.

He placed a big log in the fireplace. "Can I get you anything?"

"No, thank you. Will you please sit down?"

Taking the chair across, he watched her play with the edge of the blanket, her face flushed from crying. Staring at the burning fire, she opened her mouth to say something then refrained. She brought her legs from under the blanket to the floor, bent forward and rested her elbows on her knees. Pulling her hair back with both hands, she kept them at her nape and whispered, "There is more. Or would you rather I stop?"

CHAPTER 13

LIGHTNING

Adam moved to the couch. He put his hand on Yasmeen's shoulder. "You can tell me anything you want."

She sat back, tucked her hands between her legs. He dropped his hand and braced himself for what she was struggling to say.

"Zai . . . Zainab and I graduated from college together." Yasmeen's voice trembled. "She was more courageous than I am and spoke her mind freely. It was Fadi's effect on her, I think. They planned to get engaged at the end of the year. Did you know that?"

Adam didn't know if she expected an answer. The look on her face told him she wasn't even aware he was there.

"I didn't know," he said after a few moments of silence.

She blinked a couple of times, as if his words brought her back from wherever she went to in her head.

"When the uprising broke in March, Zainab's father was arrested on his way home from a demonstration. My father insisted she and her mother come live with us until things calmed down, and he found out where her father was being held. They didn't have family in Damascus. But things got worse. More men disappeared or were arrested by the army."

"Army? Not the police?"

"There was no difference. One day in July, I went with Mother to check on a friend of the family. Her son was killed by a sniper. Zainab and her mother stayed home. The police did a neighborhood sweep and arrested Zainab that day." Yasmeen went quiet, her breathing shallow and her hands still.

Adam placed his hand on hers and gave it a squeeze.

"Before the uprising took full effect, the police arrested the female relatives of wanted men and kept them in neighborhood clinics until their male relatives turned themselves in. It was a matter of honor, and the police knew how to play that card. At the time, both Fadi and my father were involved in coordination efforts of the opposition. They kept moving from one hiding place to another, and we could not inform them of her arrest fast enough."

She turned toward him, hair spilling over her shoulders, eyes wide and glassy. "I helped Zainab's mother pick her up piece by piece from our door step every morning for four days. They delivered her legs in a plastic bag on the first day. They rang the doorbell and left them there. The shoes she borrowed from me the morning she was taken were still on her feet."

"Dear God in Heaven."

Yasmeen closed her eyes. More tears ran down. "There are no words to describe her mother's scream that morning. They sent her arms the next day, her body the morning after. Mother and I tried to stop her from going to the door every time, but she would not listen."

"She must've had a tiny hope the body parts didn't belong to her daughter."

Yasmeen lifted wet eyelashes. "But it *was* Zainab.

Her head arrived on the fourth day. We emptied our refrigerator to store the body pieces until we found a way to inform the men. It was big enough, similar to the white one in your kitchen."

His eyes flew toward the kitchen, then back again to Yasmeen's ghost-like face.

"Zainab was finally put together for her burial. We buried her under the orange tree in our courtyard. She always wanted to live in our house, now she will forever stay there." She snatched tissues from the coffee table and blew into them. "The news reached Fadi that same day. He took me across the Turkish border that night. Mother stayed with Zainab's mother until Father could take them to her family in Jordan."

What could he say to someone who'd gone through such a horror? He took Yasmeen in his arms. "I'm so sorry."

A jasmine petal caught in her hair fell into his lap.

"So sorry, sweetheart."

"Yesterday, for a few minutes, I was in our neighborhood clinic in my mind. I thought I was going to be chopped up like Zainab." Yasmeen sobbed. "I keep hearing her mother's piercing cry in my head. Every time I open the refrigerator door, I hold my breath, even though my mind knows Zainab's body parts are not there."

"Those bastards," he muttered under his breath and kept repeating the same words over and over. "I'm so sorry."

"I was the one who they were supposed to arrest. They wanted me so Fadi would turn himself in. I am his sister. That was the message."

His throat muscles tightened, making it difficult

to swallow, like the day bees stung him when he was a boy. "I know this's hard for you, but it's not your fault." He touched her cheek. "Hush, sweetheart."

"You think it was easy for a devoted brother like Fadi to send his sister with a stranger? To throw away all traditions and religious rules so easily? He had no choice. *I* had no choice." She buried her face in his chest, her body giving in to uncontrollable release.

In time, she stopped crying and Adam felt her body lose its tension. He helped her go upstairs to her room, laid her on her bed. She tugged at the front of his shirt, pulling him down with her. Perched on the edge of the bed, he looked into her red eyes and tried to read her message in their depth.

She tugged his shirt again.

Moving with caution, he stretched on his back, tucked one hand under his head and kept the other by his side.

Yasmeen tensed, snatched her hands off his shirt, and turned them into fists under her chin.

"You want me to leave?"

"No," she whispered. "Could you stay until I fall asleep without . . . without expecting more?"

"You have my word." How could she think he might expect anything of her in the state she was in, with images in his head of what she'd had described? Didn't she figure out what sort of man he was yet?

Yasmeen curled against him, using his shoulder for a pillow. He inhaled her intoxicating cent. Her knee rubbed against his thigh a couple of times before she settled. He counted to ten, then released his breath.

Concentrating on a crack in the ceiling, he went over her story, coming up with things he could have said instead of mumbling how sorry he was. He could have told her he understood what it felt like to suffer in silence at a young age. He could have said he was glad she wasn't in the house when they arrested her friend, that she was spared, that she was here in his house sleeping in his arms. There was no way he could tell her about her father now. She knew too much about what happened to those who got arrested.

What if he fell asleep, had another nightmare and attacked her again? That would be the end of her, for sure. What if he fell asleep, had a different kind of dream and acted on it? Would she welcome him? What was he thinking? How long had it been since he was invited to a woman's bed and accepted? Too damn long.

The hand cradling his head started to go numb. Stretching his arm to the side, he tried to relieve the numbness. Good, that should keep him alert. His shoulder jerked and Yasmeen readjusted her head, spilling flower-scented hair on his face. Oh, hell.

He grabbed the mattress sheets behind her back with his now tingling hand and pushed the runaway strands aside with his other hand. The tips of his fingers brushed her neck.

She let out a murmur.

A quiver ran through his body. He retracted his hand, closed his eyes, and imagined himself shoveling cow manure into a bin, counting the number of trips it took him to transfer the pile. The surge of his desire for her simmered around ninety trips. How could he be turned on at a time like this? What the hell was wrong with him?

He tried to imagine a young Yasmeen in her special room with hands on her ears attempting to block the terrifying screams of men she admired, her whole body curled under a blanket.

Parts of her body appeared in the picture. Her tiny waist just a couple of inches away from his hand, her smooth legs being revealed by a pulled-up nightgown, her breasts pressed against him in an embrace. His body refused to cooperate with his efforts to keep his word to her. He needed to get away.

Yasmeen's breathing was steady. She'd fallen into a deep sleep. He extracted his limbs from hers as smooth as he could and walked out. A cold shower would enable him to regain some self-respect and, with any luck, maybe he could fall asleep the rest of the night.

***

Yasmeen stepped into a green training suit with her hair still wet, feeling clean inside and out. A hot shower energized her in a special way, as if the water gave her new skin. Last night's interaction with Adam, his tenderness and understanding, washed her inner soul. She felt untainted this morning, undamaged, almost physically lighter, as if sharing the burden of Zainab's memory with Adam took off a little weight. Adam told her it was not her fault. Could he really believe that? If he did, maybe she could believe it too. The restful sleep she had was incomparable. Was it because of the relief she achieved by talking about it? Or was it because of him, physically being there, lending her his strength, his warmth, and his acceptance?

Brushing her hair, she smiled at her audacity in

inviting him to lay beside her, something she could not have imagined herself doing in a million years. Did Mother not tell her that a good, upright woman would not explicitly beckon her man? A good wife needed only to hint at desire, a good husband should understand, and the rest would be taken care of by nature? Adam asked her if she wanted him to stay last night, and she was thankful he did. Maybe it was a cultural thing she needed to get used to.

If she stayed longer.

If she was a real wife.

Invited by mouthwatering aromas, she skipped downstairs. Adam cooked breakfast at the stove, his back to her. He wore tan corduroy pants and a long sleeve tee-shirt the color of his hair. She should find a way to tell him the color did not suit him, maybe go shopping for clothes for him soon.

"Good morning."

Adam turned, winced and grabbed his leg in the process. He tried to cover it with a smile. "You look rested."

"What is the expression? I slept like a child." She moved closer and looked into the skillet on the stove.

"Slept like a baby," he corrected.

"Thank you. For everything." Her tone guaranteed he understood she meant it.

"You're welcome."

She noticed the new refrigerator then, standing shorter than the old one and reflecting a bright yellow color. "What is this?"

"Thought the Abeldeens would get better use of a bigger fridge. We swapped."

"It does not go with the kitchen."

"They have weird taste, but I can get used to it." He tipped his head toward her. "Can you?"

Tears stung her eyes. "I am sure I can." Trying to catch her breath, she sat at the table and fingered the placemat. "I do not know what to say."

"Don't say anything." He brought her a plate and brushed her cheek with the back of his finger. "Just eat and get better."

She watched him throughout the meal. He seemed preoccupied and avoided making eye contact. Maybe she should give him a break from her company. The past few days have been difficult for him too.

"I think I will go for my walk this afternoon, stop to thank Mrs. Abeldeen for the food she brought. I will bake her something and return her casserole."

"First we've got to stop by the clinic to change the wound dressing and check on your stitches. You think you'll be alright with that? I could ask Rose to come out here if you prefer, but I really want Doc to look at it."

"Going to the clinic is fine with me." She wiped her mouth with her napkin. "I will bake something for Rose too, to thank her for her trouble."

"She was doing her job."

"I know, but I would feel better if I did. Do you mind?"

"Just don't exert yourself. I'll help you prepare something for the evening too. My friend Jonathan and his girlfriend plan to visit, if it's okay with you?"

Yasmeen clapped her hands. "We are going to have visitors?"

Adam flashed a beautiful smile. "Don't you think it's time we do?"

CHAPTER 14

A BREEZE

"That was heavenly delicious, Jasmine. You've got to give me the recipe." Amy carried dessert plates into the kitchen.

Yasmeen worked on the coffee machine. She gave up on correcting Amy about the right pronunciation of her name after the fourth time. "I will write the recipe for you. I am not good using American measurements."

"I'll figure it out. Jonathan loved it." Amy peered over her shoulder. "Add three more scoops in there. We like our coffee strong."

"I don't understand how you call this coffee." She threw her hands up in the air. "I can't get used to it. If only I had a way to make Turkish coffee."

"What does it take?" Amy licked her fingers with thin colorless lips after her pink lipstick had been worn away.

"The coffee beans need to be ground like powder with cardamom."

"Like an espresso fine grind? Jonathan can

make you a special bean grinder if you tell him the specifics." Amy opened cabinet doors one by one. "Oh my God! It's like a picture from a house-decorating magazine here. Do you use a ruler to make everything line up like that?"

Yasmeen smiled to herself. Adam used a mental ruler when he placed the dishes and cups on the shelves.

"What are you looking for?"

"Sugar bowl."

"To your left."

Amy put the sugar bowl on a tray. "Of course, we can always order the grinder online, but Jonathan likes to make things out of the junk piled in his shop. It'd be great if you give him the chance." She shook her head. "No idea what the other thing is."

"Cardamom is a spice." She appreciated Amy's desire to help. "But it is really not necessary."

"Don't know much about exotic spices."

Some people could be immediately warmed up to, and Amy was one of them. When she walked in earlier this evening, she had given Yasmeen a thorough look, hugged her then declared they would become good friends. Her bubbly personality filled the room with natural joy and laughter. It made Yasmeen feel older though they were only a year apart.

Amy hurried ahead of her to the living room carrying the coffee tray, her straight blond hair swinging. She wore a leopard print dress and brown boots. Amy's choice for the dress matched her personality. This could turn into a good friendship. They seemed to be on opposite ends of a personality scale. Did opposites not attract?

***

Adam switched on the flood light outside the barn and leaned his back on the tractor, letting Jonathan check the vehicle.

"Didn't tell me she's easy on the eyes." Jonathan tried the engine.

"I don't tell you a lot of things."

"I know. Have to drag stuff outa you." Jonathan lifted the hood and started poking around.

"What's with your leg, man? Looks like you can barely stand on it tonight."

"Haven't slept much lately. It'll be okay. Just need some rest."

"Not much sleep, huh? I can see why. She has a nice ra—"

"Watch it," Adam threatened, keeping his tone playful.

"Yeah, yeah. I get it. We're talkin' about your wife. I won't go there. Did you find out what she meant by her strange statement?"

"Yup."

"Gonna tell me?"

"Nope."

Jonathan's head popped up behind one side of the hood. "Come on, man. Don't leave me hangin'."

He shook his head. "None of your business."

"Can you at least tell me if it's what you suspected?"

He straightened and faced his friend. "Drop it."

"Fine." Jonathan's head disappeared again. "What about the legal stuff? You shouldn't wait too long."

"I know, I know." He pushed his hands in his jacket pockets. "I'm looking for the right moment to bring it up. You know this's the first time I've seen her relaxed? Don't think she let herself laugh out loud before tonight. Amy's a Godsend."

"I don't think it's Amy's effect alone." Jonathan closed the hood with a loud thud. "There's somethin' in the way Jasmine looks at you when you don't know she's lookin'."

"How?"

"Not a totally innocent look's all I can say. Somethin' happen between you two since we last talked?"

He wasn't sure how to phrase what happened last night. "We reached an understanding. I'm fine with it. Stop worrying."

"Understandin', my ass." Jonathan placed his hands on the hood and leaned forward. "Make a move."

"It's not that simple. She's . . . different."

"You can say that again," Jonathan mumbled under his breath.

"Can't figure out what she wants."

"You're rusty from lack of practice, my friend. How long since Jessica dumped you? Fifteen years?"

"Four, jackass. Look, Yasmeen's starting to trust me. Don't want to ruin things."

Jonathan motioned for him to start the engine. He slid behind the wheel. It protested a couple of times and then roared its normal running noise. He turned it off after Jonathan gave him the signal.

"I'm a magician," Jonathan beamed. "Let's get back. Shouldn't leave the women alone. Knowin' Amy, she'll find a way to tell Jasmine every detail about your past crap."

"That's a short sentence," Adam joked, following him up the front steps.

Jonathan held the door handle before he opened

it. "Do yourself a favor, will you?"

"What?" Adam braced for it.

"Give yourself more of a chance with this one. I like her."

***

As soon as the men left the house, Amy scooted next to Yasmeen on the couch.

"Tell me the truth now. How did you really hook Adam? Almost every single woman in town tried and failed. A few married women too."

Yasmeen knew this question was coming, and she prepared an answer based on what Adam had told her to say. But maybe she could avoid telling a lie, or half the truth as Adam had phrased it, if she diverted Amy's attention to something else. She peered sideways at Amy.

"Including Maryanne Merick?"

Amy fell for it. "You know about her, huh?"

"How hard did she try?"

"Very, very hard. Used to visit his mother. Pretended to be her friend just to get close to Adam and flirt with him. Tried harder after he broke up with Jessica." Amy raised her eyebrows. "You do know about Jessica?"

She had no idea who Jessica was, but the

situation called for some encouragement and prodding. "Somewhat."

"Adam was lonely after Jessica. Didn't fall in Maryanne's trap, though." Amy gave a soft laugh. "She never gave up. He used to escape into town whenever she came to visit his mother. Jonathan and I knew, whenever we saw Adam in town in the middle of the day, Maryanne was paying an announced visit."

Amy nibbled on crackers and fruits from a plate on the coffee table. "After Mrs. Shipman passed away, there was no excuse. Couldn't openly go after him without her husband taking notice."

"How did Adam treat her?" Yasmeen caught herself hanging on Amy's words, impatient for the time Amy took to savor a ripe strawberry.

"He was kind. Knew she wanted him, so he kept his distance. If you ask me, he should've turned her down."

"You mean speak to her about it?"

"Some women hang on a thread unless things are spelled out for them. Once and for all, you know?"

Yasmeen nodded. She did not know, however. A situation like this was new to her.

"I told Adam to spell it out for Maryanne." Amy licked her fingers. "But he said she understood he wasn't interested. Thought there was no need to hurt her feelings. He's so nice, right?"

"He is." Yasmeen searched for another topic to keep Amy talking before she started asking her questions.

"Amy, I really do not know a lot about Jessica."

"Jessica was a big mistake, if you ask me." Amy didn't skip a beat. "Jonathan never liked her. She and Adam started dating his senior year. When he enlisted, she loved the uniform. Sent him letters and emails. Talked to him online. Stuff like that." Amy picked at the crumbs on her dress.

"What happened between them?" Yasmeen fought the urge to tap her fingers.

"The few times he came home on leave, Jessica was all over him the first couple of days. After that she was conveniently out of town for one family emergency or another every time he came home. He told Jonathan he never suspected it was deliberate."

"What does that word mean?" She hated to interrupt but she needed to understand.

"Deliberate? It means on purpose. You know, to avoid being with him."

"Being with him," she repeated, hoping Amy would explain further without her having to ask. Did that mean they lived together?

Amy pursed her lips to one side and squinted,

giving her a quizzical look. "You understand?"

"Yes." She would not ask. Better not to know.

"When he left the army and came home, they dated for about a month then she dumped him. Said she didn't like the man he'd become. That's what she told him. Can you imagine that? She didn't even *like* him anymore."

"Does he see her in town? It must be difficult for him."

"Jessica took off to New York. Wanted to leave farm and small-town life at any price. Some women are not cut out for this place. Not enough excitement."

Amy shook her head. "Not me. I want to raise my children on the same land I grew up on. How do you like it here so far?"

"I come from a big city. Granted it has a different culture, but Damascus has the same kind of excitement and distractions as any other. Here, it is peaceful, quiet and healthy." She tried to be honest, wishing to get back to the topic of Jessica. "I like the people I have met so far. I doubt I would like Jessica even if Adam was out of the picture."

"If only she was honest, he might've handled it better. She said one thing to his face, and another behind his back. I bet he didn't tell you that about her, huh?"

Before Yasmeen could answer, Amy continued, "That's Adam for you. He'd never say anything bad about anyone. He's the type who keeps things inside. Jonathan thinks it's because of what his dad did to him." Amy did a double take to check with Yasmeen. "Please tell me you know about his dad."

She repeated Adam's own words. "He was an animal."

"Didn't know the man, but I know some stories Jonathan told me of Adam's childhood. You know they were friends since first grade?"

"They have a special relationship."

"That's an understatement. I get jealous sometimes, but then I remember that Jonathan's the only friend Adam has. Do you have a special friend like that back home?"

She took several seconds to absorb the question. When she spoke, her voice was subdued. "I used to."

"Never lived anywhere but here. Don't know what it's like to be far away with everything unfamiliar. If you'll let me, I'll be a good friend to you. I'm a good listener and I'm honest." Amy gave her a genuine smile. "I'll tell you to your face if you screw up, you can count on that."

Yasmeen returned the smile. "I will not accept anything less."

"I'll start right now, then. You've made a horrible mistake."

"What did I do?"

"You had Adam buy you my ring."

"Excuse me?"

"I kept my eye on that ring in Mr. Polensky's shop for two years. Adam beat Jonathan to it."

"Amy, I am not sure I understand."

"I have to pick another ring now. When Jonathan proposes, that is. I could push him into it." Amy raised her fingers and wiggled them in Yasmeen's face in a quotation gesture. "Accidently get pregnant." She lowered her hands and placed them on her chest. "But I'm not selfish enough to skip my pills, and like I said, I'm honest."

Yasmeen could not determine if Amy was serious or if she was joking.

CHAPTER 15

A MESSAGE

Adam lounged in his armchair and welcomed a powerful yawn, neglecting to hide it behind his closed fist. He was exhausted. Jonathan ushered Amy out the door, calling the evening over.

Following Yasmeen to the kitchen, he helped her clean up, his eye on the clock. He had a number of things to take care of in the morning, and he needed to rise earlier than usual to get them done.

Yasmeen talked about the evening, cheerful and excited. Although he was dead tired, her happy mood lifted his spirits.

"It is a pity they are not married." Yasmeen brought him a stack of dishes to wash. "They seem to be happy together."

He yawned again. His hands covered with soap bubbles, he couldn't cover his gaping mouth if he tried. "Jonathan's not ready to take that step yet."

"But they live together, right? Like husband and wife?" Yasmeen placed plates in the sink, not meeting his eyes. "She talked about things only a …

married woman would talk about."

He coughed into his fist to cover his surprise. Soap bubbles shot out and floated around her head. "What do you mean? Things like what?"

"Private things. I am not going to tell you. But my point is why does Jonathan not marry Amy and make it official? She wants to be married. She wants children too."

He ran his hands under running water and dried them. Exhausted from lack of sleep and succumbing to physical pain, his leg muscles started to spasm. He rubbed his eyes with the heels of his hands. "A man shouldn't be pressured into marriage. Has to come when he's good and ready, or else he'll regret it." He lowered his hands and was struck to see Yasmeen with a horrified look on her face, all joyfulness gone.

"I am sorry you had to be in such a position." Her words fell flat. "I hope it will not last for long and I go back soon."

"This has nothing to do with you and me. God, I didn't mean to offend you. I'm so tired I don't know what I'm saying." He moved closer. "I made the decision to marry you. You were the one who was pressured into this, not me. You told me that yourself."

She backed away. "Be honest. If it were not for

my brother, you would be a free man." She walked out of the kitchen and darted upstairs.

The slam of her bedroom door pulsed through the house, like a whip snapping at him. He held the back of a chair and leaned on it, relieving his aching leg from the weight of his body. He uttered every curse he knew under his breath. Shoving the chair aside, he limped upstairs, knocked on her door.

Yasmeen yanked the door open and fixed her eyes on his chest. "Before you say anything, I want you to know that I am actually very grateful to you. It was a nice normal day today, I forgot the reality of our situation and you reminded me. So, I became angry for no reason. I have been too emotional lately." Her voice dropped. "We both know why. I apologize for overreacting."

He observed her attempt to explain away the hurt she felt, like she did when he attacked her before. His mother used to do that with his father too. Was it a woman thing, a survival skill? To avoid more harm?

"Yasmeen, look at me please."

With a shaky breath, she did.

"If it weren't for your brother, my mother would have buried her only son, and I wouldn't be standing here asking your forgiveness."

A tear rolled down and collected at the bottom

of her chin. He used his index finger to lift the teardrop. "Before you came into my life, I was content alone, knowing I'm no prize." He licked his finger, tasted its saltiness on his tongue. The act must have surprised her, seeing her lips part with an audible inhale.

"Now, I wish I was a different man, one you'd choose on your own." His leg buckled. He held the doorframe on each side and buried his face in his arm. "Need to sit down." He clenched teeth. "My leg . . . cramping."

Yasmeen wrapped her arms around his waist and helped him onto her bed. She squatted at his feet and pulled his boots off.

He clutched his thigh with both hands in agony.

"Is there medicine you need to take?" She helped him lay back on the bed and stretch his legs.

"My nightstand," he managed between breaths.

She ran out, returning with the pill bottle and a glass of water. "Would a heat compress help?"

His hand shook taking the pills. Sweat broke out all over his body. "This'll work in a few minutes."

She sat on the edge of the bed. "How about if I massage it?"

He clenched his jaw and shot her skeptical look.

"Don't worry. I will be gentle." She placed the glass on the nightstand and pushed his chest until he was flat on his back. "Just relax."

Yasmeen worked her fingers in slow motion to his calf and back again, changing pressure and compressing the flesh under the fabric of his pants.

He couldn't help the grunts of pain that escaped him. He overlapped his forearms on his damp forehead, inhaled through his nose and exhaled through his mouth in an attempt to absorb the pain. He listened to Yasmeen's breathing rhythm and tried to match it to distract himself from his misery.

In time, the pills took effect, and the efforts of her fingers brought him a measure of relief. The pain dissipated. Adam's mind shifted focus, his body responding to her hands in an entirely different manner, somewhat joyful.

Yasmeen inched one hand under his thigh and worked her thumb in circles. "Is this because of an injury you had at war?"

He lowered his arms to his sides. "Aha."

"Where exactly?"

"Two bullets near the hip."

Her other hand inched closer to the injury sight. "That was your only wound?"

"Left shoulder and arm." He looked for something to grab with his hands and clutched fistfuls of the bed sheet. "Those bullet wounds healed faster. Didn't leave permanent damage." Did she know the effect she was having on him? Could she be this clueless? Or was this intentional?

"Could've been worse if it weren't for your brother."

Yasmeen's hands turned their attention to the lower part of his thigh, above the knee.

He began counting manure piles in his head. Control. He needed to stay in control.

"I wanted to ask you about your limp when I first saw you, but I did not know how." She threw him a quick look. "I did not want to embarrass you."

"Why would I get embarrassed?"

"I did not want to hurt your pride."

He watched her hair hang close over his right fist. "It happened while I served my country. I'm proud of that, at the very least."

"Hmm," was all she uttered while her fingers kept working wonders. She bent sideways to move his other leg out of the way. Her hair brushed the back of his fist.

He sucked in a sharp breath and held it for a short while. He should tell her to stop before the situation became uncontrollable. "Where did you learn how to do this?"

"My grandmother taught me. Ever since I was little, I worked on her, and then I practiced on my mother. She said I have magical fingers."

Adam exhaled long and loud. "I agree."

She adjusted her position on the bed. Her hip touched his thigh.

"Stop!"

She hurried off the bed. "Did I hurt you?"

"No, no. It was good." He rose upright and swung his legs down.

Yasmeen placed her hands on his shoulders. "You should not stand on it yet."

Adam gripped the edge of the mattress with both hands, his head level with her chest. His eyes caught the second button of her blouse straining to hold the fabric folds together. "I need to go." He cleared his throat. "Now."

She stepped aside.

He pushed himself off the bed and limped to the door.

"Adam?"

He turned, his heart about to bruise his ribs. Did she really say his name? Or did he take too many pills, and he was hearing things now?"

"Just so you know," her voice quivered. "I do not wish you to be a different man."

He swallowed. *Make a move*, Jonathan's voice commanded in his head.

CHAPTER 16

AN EXPERIMENT

Adam took a step toward her.

Yasmeen took one back and hit the nightstand. "Good night."

"Don't play games with me, Yasmeen." His voice came out harsh, despite his intent to be considerate. "I deserve better than that."

She pushed hair away from her face. "I am not playing games."

"Did you mean what you said?"

"Yes. I think you deserve for me to be as honest as possible." She inched around the nightstand and backed up to the wall. "Why are you making a mountain out of this?"

He closed the distance between them. "You can't say things like that to a man and ask him to walk away." He pointed to the bed. "You can't touch me the way you just did and not expect a reaction."

She lifted her chin. "I have been nothing but

trouble for you since I arrived. Now that I found something I could actually help you with, you get angry with me."

He placed one palm on the wall by her head. "I'm not angry."

"What do you call this, then?"

"Thought you knew how the world works. Take a guess."

She turned her head sideways. Strands of her hair stuck to the rough wall. "You are making me uncomfortable."

He leaned closer, enough for him to feel the heat emanating from her skin. "Join the club."

She frowned. "What club?"

He released a frustrated breath. "Will you please look at me?"

She turned her head to face him, placed both palms on his chest. "I am not certain what just happened. I was simply trying to help. Could you please leave now?"

Her hands trembled through the fabric of his shirt, there was a tremor in her voice and when she looked at him, he read something different in her eyes. Innocence?

"You sure that's what you want?"

She nodded, her face and neck flushed.

He pulled back, retreated to his room and shut

the door. Facing his window, he leaned his forehead on the cold glass. He didn't expect her reaction. She was scared, and he cornered her, tested her innocence. Why did he let this happen? He pulled his shirt over his head and flung it to a corner. Damn his sluggish mind, damn his bum leg, damn his pills and Goddamn Jonathan to hell for screwing with his head.

Yasmeen slid to the floor and hugged her knees. She shook from head to toe and her chest felt tight. She could not take her eyes off Adam's boots by the bed. How did she get to this point? Why did she not think it through before she put her hands on him? Stupid, stupid woman. She shifted her eyes to the door and threw her head back. What had she done? What if he came back? What would she say?

Straightening, she smoothed the front of her shirt and picked up Adam's boots. She opened her door and placed them in front of his closed door, careful not to make a sound. Back in her room, she put her hand on the door locks and paused. Adam would not come in. He would not try anything indecent. He was a man of his word, promised Fadi he would not force her into anything. Promised her, too.

Letting go of the unturned lock, she stepped

away from the door. Why was she panting? Adam's closeness planted something inside her, something physical, intimidating. She dropped down on her bed. Was she scared by his attentions?

Be honest with yourself, her father's words echoed in her head. No. She knew what fear felt like, paralyzing her body, holding her mind hostage with panic. No. This was different, new. This was appealing. More frightening.

* * *

Adam intended to leave the house before Yasmeen emerged from her room in the morning. No such luck. He found her waiting for him in the kitchen.

She prepared him a cup of coffee and set it at the place opposite to hers on the table.

"We need to talk."

He shoved his hands in his pants pockets and stayed by the entrance. "Look, about last night. I wasn't myself." He shifted his weight from foot to foot. "Pain and pills clouded my judgment."

"I am not—" She snatched a napkin off the table. "I do not know how to do this."

"Do what?

"Be here, with you, without you taking it the

wrong way."

Adam looked out the window. Dawn barely broke the skyline. It wouldn't be wrong, he wanted to tell her, but her message was loud and clear. Only she didn't know she sent it.

"I jumped the gun."

"I do not know what that means."

He tapped his chest. "It's my fault."

She twisted the napkin. "We had an agreement, remember?"

"Haven't forgotten. Never meant to make you uncomfortable."

She left her chair and rounded the table to face him. "I did not know . . ." her face turned bright red. "You had those feelings."

"I'm a normal man with a healthy appetite, Yasmeen." He tapped the side of his damaged thigh with his hand. "Don't let this fool you."

Shreds of the napkin fluttered to the floor. "I am sorry."

He headed to the back door. "Last night was a huge misunderstanding. Let's forget it. Can you do that for me?"

She nodded, tears glistening in her eyes. "Can you?"

"Don't worry. It won't happen again." He hoped he could keep that promise.

CHAPTER 17

A DANCE

A blizzard dumped the first snow of the season. There was nothing gradual about this winter. One day the cows grazed in the pasture; the next, everything was white and buried under inches of snow.

Adam prepared well for this day. The free-stall housings were ready for his herd, the feed mixed and waiting to be dispensed, the milking parlors equipped with pipelines, and the weekly schedule for collecting manure in lined bins was set. He always took the first shift, hating every second of the task, shoveling nitrogen rich, repugnant, yet valuable, manure twice a day into storage. When he lived alone, he didn't mind it that much as he endured the stench until he scrubbed himself clean at the end of the day. But with Yasmeen around, he needed to keep his distance, find a way to wash and change clothes before he returned home to spare her his nauseating smell. His only option was the hose behind the barn. Stripping and washing in cold water every afternoon was painful but necessary before he entered the house and headed straight for a hot shower.

Yasmeen was unaware of his daily struggles. She seemed to enjoy her new friendship with Amy and spent most of her free time with her. They went into town often, and she met more people. He noticed how Yasmeen tried to pick up the American accent, but some expressions still threw her off. He found it endearing, somewhat amusing.

She started giving the youngest Abeldeen child art classes upon her mother's request. Mrs. Abeldeen had complained that her four-year old was behind with her language skills. Yasmeen explained there were many forms of communication and perhaps, some training in artwork would give the child a different tool of expression. They tried a couple of sessions. Little Sara showed interest and class times were set.

Yasmeen and Sara worked on the kitchen table every day, using many ingredients to be creative. Filling the house with noise and activity, it was clear to him Yasmeen appreciated the chance to have a schedule, to wake up every morning with a mission in mind, feeling useful and needed.

Jonathan surprised her one afternoon with the coffee grinder, and it became a ritual for Adam to enjoy a cup of strong Turkish coffee with Yasmeen after dinner. She asked detailed questions about farm tasks and sometimes, requested to see particular activities.

He did what he could to show her around, shielding her from the most undesirable tasks of managing his farm in the cold weather. It seemed to him she was making the effort to fit into his life, maybe accepting her fate, however temporary. He admired the ease with which she took Sara under her wing. Their daily lessons brought a measure of normalcy and warmth to the house. It made him jealous at some basic level.

He contacted Jonathan's cousin in Milwaukee and had him prepare the necessary papers for Yasmeen's residency application. He planned to approach her about it as soon as the forms arrive in the mail and explain to her his legal responsibility to move forward with the process.

One cold afternoon, he returned to the house earlier than usual. Another snowstorm was on its way and he felt it in his bones. He walked in the kitchen door to the sounds of Sara's laughter. Loud music played from the living room, classical with violins and piano sounds. He took off his boots, hung his thick jacket by the door and rounded the corner.

Her back to him, Yasmeen was dancing. Her body swayed with the music like a corn stalk ruffled by soft wind, arms extended above her head, and hands twirling in the air. Her hair swayed left and right in opposite directions of her hips. She wore a long ruffled black skirt and a tight red tee-shirt, her feet bare.

"Like a flowing fountain, Sara." She laughed, a pure, unreserved, hearty laugh.

He shifted his eyes to the little girl by the window. Sara giggled and moved in an obvious attempt to mimic Yasmeen. He leaned his back to the wall and drank in the scene. The beat of the music slowed and dwindled to one instrument, perhaps a flute. Yasmeen held the hem of her skirt, lifted it and fluttered it to her sides.

"Butterflies." She dipped and swung across the room. Sara followed.

His heart danced in his chest. He wished he could stand there undetected until he had his fill. He knew the instant Yasmeen saw him, her attitude would take a dramatic change.

She turned, her eyes landed on him and stumbled to a stop. Her cheeks healthy red, her chest heaving up and down with the labor of exercise. The rhythm of the music picked up speed with the sounds of drums in the background.

Lifting his palms in a defensive move, he opened his mouth to come up with some kind of apology, though he didn't feel one bit sorry.

"Hortheth!" Sara squeaked.

Yasmeen looked at the excited girl. "That is right. It sounds like running horses." She extended her arms and hopped toward him, held his hands and tugged him off the wall, galloping backwards.

Following her lead, he stomped his feet and thought of motions he could make to be convincing as a horse, he sure smelled like one too. Throwing his head back, he neighed like an idiot, feeling self-conscious and totally lost.

They swept through the living room, following Sara's bouncing body. They went into the kitchen and circled the table a couple of times, all the while laughing and making animal sounds that had nothing to do with horses.

The music stopped. They collapsed around the kitchen table, out of breath. Sara pulled the chair to Adam's right and tried to climb on it. She tripped on her long skirt. Adam lifted her to sit her on the table instead.

Yasmeen bent at the waist, her skin glistening with perspiration. She threw her arms forward and reached to hold Sara's feet.

"Would you please get Sara a juice box from the fridge?" She winked at him. "Earnest."

"Earnest could learn a thing or two from his master."

He turned to the fridge and grabbed three juice boxes. He inserted the straw in one box, handed it to Sara, and threw one to Yasmeen across the table. She stopped it from sliding off the side with her hip.

"How come you are home this early?"

"It's going to turn nasty out there." He sucked on the straw of his juice box, coughed, and dripped yellow liquid down his shirt. "What the he—" he caught himself and coughed some more. "What's this?"

Yasmeen laughed again, that ringing musical sound. "Apple juice." She watched Sara, completely absorbed with the task of finishing her drink. "Her favorite."

Adam studied Yasmeen's glowing face, her eyes warm and mellow. It was a side he hadn't seen of her before, the happy, almost childish-like side. A knock on the door diverted his attention.

"That's your daddy, Sara." Yasmeen helped her jump to the floor. "Let's put on your coat and boots and I will see you tomorrow."

Ben stood inside by the door and waited for his daughter to get ready. He handed Adam a bundle of envelopes. "Picked up the mail for you."

"Thanks." He examined the big manila envelope from the attorney, Sam.

"Gonna be a bad one, tonight. Everythin' ready? You need me to check the stalls again before I turn in?"

"I took care of things. Go home, Ben. Be careful."

After Ben and Sara left, Yasmeen went about the business of putting things back where they belonged. Adam followed her around.

"What was that all about? The fountain and the butterflies. The horse bit?"

"Dance is a form of art that doesn't need language. I thought it might open Sara's senses and imagination." She pointed for him to help her return the coffee table to its place in the middle of the room.

"Thank you for joining us, the way you did." She tapped his shoulder as she passed him. "It would have made Sara doubt herself if you hadn't." She bent down to pick up a couple of pillows off the floor, and the back of her tee-shirt revealed a strip of skin at her waist. "You have artistic tendencies, Adam Wegener."

Thinking of other forms of expression that didn't require language, he ran his hands over his face a couple of times while she had her back to him. He went into the kitchen, returned with the big envelope in his hands.

"There's something I need to talk to you about." He pointed to the couch. "Will you sit down, please?"

Plopping down, she placed her hands together between her knees. "What is it?"

He pulled out the stack of papers from the envelope and explained what they were. "You don't have to sign right away. We have until the end of the month to file."

"I thought I would be back home by now."

"This doesn't stop you from leaving. It just makes it legal for you to stay longer, if you wanted to. I'm not trying to trap you or anything."

"I know." She rifled through the stack.

He pointed at the yellow sticky notes scattered over the pages. "Those are the places where you're supposed to sign."

Pulling out one of the papers, she rose from the couch. "What's this?" Surprise distorted her voice.

He approached to check out what she was reading. "The application doesn't require it. But I sent Sam everything Fadi gave me in Turkey, just in case. There's nothing for you to sign there. I guess Sam sent it back for my files."

The sheet fluttered in her shaking hand. "This says you changed your religion."

"Fadi said I had to."

"Why?"

"The marriage wouldn't hold true for you if I didn't, right? Fadi didn't discard all your traditions. He didn't want you to live in sin according to your religious rules. That's how he explained it."

The shaking spread to her entire body. "I didn't know you did that."

Taking the papers from her hands, he slipped them back in the envelope. "No big deal. I'm the last person to think twice about religion, but I know it's important for your brother." He handed her the envelope.

She hugged it to her chest, tears running down, not bothering to wipe them. A couple of drops landed on the manila envelope, turning the spots brown in the several seconds that passed in silence. Why was she so affected by this?

"Do you mind if I go through the papers later?"

"No problem."

She headed to the stairs.

A dreadful void spread around Adam.

CHAPTER 18

A REPORT

Amy called Yasmeen the next morning and asked for her help planning a surprise for Jonathan's birthday.

They went into town and walked into Mrs. Dawson's Hair and Nail Salon on Main Street. Amy produced a picture from her purse, which she had cut from a magazine, and told Mrs. Dawson that she wanted her hair to look like the model's. Amy tried to entice Yasmeen to have a haircut and add highlights, but she refused. She contented herself to sit in a corner and watch Amy turn her blond hair to fiery red.

The other women in the salon talked about people she didn't know. It amused her to hear about the drunk who urinated in the middle of the street the night before, and about Mr. Beety who cheated on his wife and got caught by his mother-in-law. The women tried to include her in their conversations, and she obliged when she had something to contribute. She heard Maryanne's name mentioned a couple of times, so she talked about the clothes she bought from her store. The topic died when an older lady with short silver hair, and a green mask concealing her face, asked for advice on how to deal with her new dog's obsession with her shower curtain.

Yasmeen turned her attention to the television set, which dangled from the ceiling at an odd angle, volume muted. Why did they have it on if no one watched or listened? She read the news updates at the bottom of the screen and tried to understand a report about an American football player recovering from an injury.

World News started at the top of the hour. A handsome reporter with a dashing smile dominated the screen. The headline at the bottom of the screen read *Developing Situation in Syria*. She followed a video clip displaying scenes from a war zone, burning houses, exploding mosque minarets, wounded people running in the streets carrying more wounded people, and army tanks everywhere. The news strip reported military forces attacked cities with artillery and canons, cracking down on armed suspected terrorist groups, and that the estimated number of dead civilians that day reached one hundred and thirty.

What was going on? What armed terrorist

groups? When did peaceful demonstrations turn into a bloodbath? Who was the army fighting? What city was this? Which street was that? Dear God, was that her school?

She put her hand on her mouth to halt a scream, clamped her other hand on top of the first, and dashed out of the salon. On the sidewalk, she turned in circles, her mind processing information.

Amy rushed out. "Everything alright, Jasmine?"

"I needed to get fresh air."

Amy hooked her arm in hers. "You planning on losing your fingers and ears? You can't be out here without your winter gear."

"Are you done, Amy? Can we go home now?"

"Honey, what's wrong? You look like you've just seen a ghost. Come in before we both turn into popsicles." Amy tugged at her to get her back inside.

Her eyes flew to the television the instant she walked in. The dimpled-reporter's face was in one corner of the screen, a video of burning buildings and a city's skyline filled with smoke, played in the background.

"That's . . . my neighborhood," she whispered, her face numb.

Amy took a few seconds to understand what they were watching. "Let's get you out of here."

She rushed to help her into her winter jacket, paid Mrs. Dawson, and mumbled something about being late.

"Are you alright?" Amy took off, jerking the car forward. "Oh, Adam will be so mad at me."

Yasmeen stared outside the window, but her eyes only saw the images on the television screen.

"Why?"

"He made me promise to be careful whenever we went out. You know, not to have you hear the news or anything."

"It's not your fault. It was a ridiculous agreement between him and my brother, thinking they could shelter me like that. I was a fool to comply so far anyway."

"That video clip we saw was choppy and unclear. You're sure it was your neighborhood? How can you tell?" Amy slowed the car down. "Maybe you're mistaken? Maybe it's a different part of the country. For all I know, it might've been in Iraq."

"I saw my school. I know what I saw." She couldn't keep from screaming the words out. Closing her eyes, she breathed deep. "Please forgive me. I appreciate what you are trying to do, but I know that street. The big sign of its famous bookstore was clear." She brushed tears away. "My school was at the corner, one of the burning buildings."

"Oh, God. I don't know what to say."

Yasmeen looked outside the window again. "You know he cut the television cable and put a password on his laptop?"

"Sorry, honey. I didn't know that."

"I need that password, Amy. Give me your cell phone, please."

Amy handed over her purse. "Outside pocket. Adam's on quick dial. Just hit 6."

Waiting for Adam to accept the call, Yasmeen dug tissues from her pocket and wiped her nose. She flipped the phone closed. "He didn't answer."

"Give it to me." Amy punched another key. "Hey, babe. You know where Adam is? Tell him to go home now. He's not answering his phone. Something happened. Jasmine needs him."

Amy parked the car and was about to open her door.

Yasmeen tried a smile. "Did I tell you your hair looks nice? Sorry I ruined your plans for Jonathan's birthday."

"You haven't ruined anything." Amy touched her hair. "Come on, let's get you inside."

She laid a hand on Amy's arm. "I would like to be alone, if you don't mind."

"Are you sure? I can stay until Adam gets here."

"I will be fine. Please, don't make me feel guilty for ruining the rest of your day. Now go and do whatever it is you have planned for Jonathan. I insist."

Amy looked hesitant. "Promise you'll call if you need anything?"

"Of course." Yasmeen got out of the car. She dashed inside and fumbled with Adam's laptop on the kitchen table. She tried Jessica's name for a password. Tried again with different spellings, no luck. One after another, she tried all the names she could think of in Adam's life, including Maryanne Merick and even Gloria. Frustrated, she stared at the blinking cursor on the screen. What was his mother's first name? How come she never asked? Pounding the table with her fists, she let out angry screams.

The back door flung open with a loud thump. Adam barged in, breathing heavy. "You alright?"

"Give it to me," she shrieked.

He hurried closer. "What? What is it?"

She pointed at the laptop. "Your password. I want to know what is happening at home." She shoved his chest. "I will not follow your silly rules anymore."

He didn't budge. The expression on his face

shifted from worry to anger, or was it something else? The strange way he held her stare was odd. She didn't care to decipher it. Her entire body trembling, she wrapped her arms around her waist. "Please."

Turning to the laptop, he punched in his password. "There." He snatched paper and pen and wrote down a number. "I'll leave the password on the fridge for you."

She withdrew into her own dark world over the next few days, hardly sleeping at night and spending her daytime in her room. She studied numerous video clips of footage posted by opposition activists on the Internet, looking for a face or a name she would recognize, a street she had walked through, a shop she had frequented, or a friend's house where she had visited.

Everything was familiar yet looked foreign. When she recognized something on the screen, she sketched how it used to look before the bombings and the carnage. Shocked at the amount of escalated violence, she worried about her parents and brother, her extended family, her aunts and cousins and the many children, her friends and neighbors. She thought of the planned weddings, the expectant mothers, the scheduled graduations, the anticipated promotions and work applications, all on hold. How could life crawl forward for those who survived this lunacy? Who among them would be spared? Whom would she mourn? She went through the motions of everyday living but didn't feel alive. The only time she felt somewhat connected to reality was during Sara's lessons.

She cried. She prayed. She talked to herself like a mad woman. Sometimes, she screamed into her pillow until her lungs hurt.

Adam shouldered the mood swings with patience. When Amy told him what happened in the salon, he knew Yasmeen hacked at the dam, and the flood of information drowned her. He wished she would talk to him about it, but every time he tried to open the subject she would run to her room and shut him out. He let her have her time. If she needed the seclusion, then so be it. Let her have it. If she needed that minute measure of control, who was he to take it away from her? Just let her get past this, get back to where they were, wherever that was.

He brought dinner trays to her room every evening for a whole week. He walked around scattered papers on the floor, some sketches of faces, some of streets and buildings, and watched her sink deeper.

She kept her eyes glued to the computer screen, her hands blackened with the charcoal pencils. Every now and then, she looked at him, her face ashen, dark circles prominent under her eyes, and then returned to her preoccupation of hunting for news of home.

Deep in the night, he heard her cry. Soft steady weeping sometimes, muffled agonizing screams other times. He tried once to hold her in his arms and ease her pain. "Let me help you."

Yasmeen flinched as if his hands scorched her, moved out of his reach. "You can't fix this."

Most times, he stood in the doorway at the early hours of the day, before dawn broke, and watched her sleep. When he had to work, he returned to the house several times during the day to check on her, urging her to eat a couple of bites. He managed the house chores as well, suppressing his obsessive struggle to have things in order, knowing Yasmeen herself was not.

Walking in on her one day, he found her sitting on her knees on the floor, her back to the door, reading from a book. She had a scarf wrapped around her head. He retreated, suspecting she didn't sense his intrusion. At last, questions in the back of his mind regarding her faith were answered. The doubts he had earlier about Yasmeen not performing her religious obligations around him were confirmed.

She practiced her faith in private.

***

Amy visited a couple of times. Adam hoped she would draw Yasmeen out of the shell she had retreated into. Amy's failure disappointed him and caused him to worry even more. On the evening of her last visit, Amy left Yasmeen's room and went downstairs. He and Jonathan waited in the living room.

"I have an idea." Amy sat on the couch's arm. "You need to get her out of here."

He ran a hand through his hair. "Tried. She's not in the mood to go out."

"I mean get her out of town. Take her to Chicago. Let her feel the big city for a few days. Everywhere she turns here, she sees emptiness. She needs normalcy. Life on the farm is not the city life she's used to."

"She told you that?"

"All she said to me was not to worry, that she'd be fine."

"What would I say? Why would we go to Chicago?"

"Oh, for fuck's sake!" Jonathan exploded. "Tell her you have business there. Better yet, tell her *you* need a break from work. Take her to a play or a museum, some sappy artsy event. I don't know. Give her somethin' she can connect to. Distract her. God knows you could use an outlet too."

"You think she'd agree to go?" He tried to keep the excitement out of his voice.

"She'd do it for you. If you tell her you need the trip." Amy headed to the kitchen. "I'll make coffee."

Jonathan scooted forward in his seat. "Lay a guilt trip on her. She owes you big. Use it to your advantage."

He leapt out of his chair. "Don't want to *guilt* her into anything." He walked to the fireplace, put his hands on the mantle and looked into the flames. "I want her to heal, to recover."

Jonathan approached him and laid his hand on the back of his shoulder. "It came out wrong. Sorry, man."

Adam closed his eyes. "I'm tired of trying all the time."

"I know." Jonathan tightened his grasp.

"I think I've become too attached."

"I know."

"She wants to leave. Hasn't signed the papers

Sam sent yet." He turned to Jonathan. "Obviously, she prefers going back to a war zone than staying with me."

Jonathan held him by the shoulders. "That's not true. She doesn't know how you feel. Tell her. Show her. Do somethin'." He gave him a gentle shove. "Fight for what you want, man."

Adam took a few steps back and ran his hands through his hair. He lifted his eyes to the framed document of his grandfather's will above the mantle, his constant reminder of the bad seed he sprang from. What if his grandfather was wrong? What if he cut his father out of the will simply to punish him for his cruelty? Not because he saw something better in Adam?

"Maybe I'm not the right man for her."

"How about you let her decide that?" Jonathan called Amy back into the room. "Pack for this weekend, babe. We're goin' to Chicago with them. We'll take my truck."

***

Adam woke up with a start. He raised his head off the pillow and listened to the distant ringing noise that penetrated his slumber. He got out of bed and stumbled over his boots in the dark. He cursed, switched on the lights, hurried to pull on his pajama pants, and headed to the hallway. He followed the sound downstairs.

Yasmeen stood between the coffee table and the couch in the living room. She had her hair gathered to one side and wore a blue nightgown that stopped short of covering her knees. She held his cell phone and stated the obvious. "You have a call."

Adam took the cell phone just as it went silent. He checked the screen. Unknown number. Stretching around Yasmeen to switch the light on the corner table, he brushed her bare arm in the process. Shivers ran down his spine.

"I usually turn it off before I go to bed. Must have raised the volume instead. Did it wake you?"

"I wasn't asleep. I was in the kitchen getting a drink when I heard—"

An incoming call interrupted her. Adam pushed the answer button. "Hello?" He waited a few seconds for a response. The caller hung up.

"Who calls this late at night?"

"Most likely a wrong number." He switched his phone to silent mode, threw it on the cushions. The light behind her penetrated the fabric of her nightgown transforming it to almost see-through material. It outlined every detail of her body. He swallowed.

"You must be freezing." He snatched the blanket off the couch and draped it around her shoulders, inserted his palms around her neck, and lifted her hair to free the trapped strands. He kept his hands on her shoulders.

Yasmeen leaned forward and rested her forehead on his chest. "I'm so tired."

"There's nothing you can do, sweetheart." He rested his chin on top of her head, inhaled that flowery scent of hers. "Let me take you away for a couple of days."

She turned her head sideways, laid her cheek flat against his bare chest. "Where?"

He caressed the back of her neck, rubbed her hair between his fingers. Silky strands slithered over his skin. "Chicago." His voice deepened. "You'll like it there. It'll get your mind off the horrible things you've been watching." The phone vibrated on the couch behind her. He ignored it. "I could use a break too."

"I don't have the energy to go anywhere. I know it is not fair to you, but I can't help it."

He wondered if she heard his heart racing under her cheek. "Do it for me, Yasmeen. I can't go on like this."

"What do you mean?"

"I'm worried about you all the time. Can hardly

work."

She pulled back. "When can we go?"

He let his hands drop to his sides. "This weekend."

"Fine. I will go." She turned toward the stairs.

He stayed behind, picked up his phone, and tried to bring his heartbeat back to normal.

CHAPTER 19

ICE

While waiting for Adam to get the truck from the parking lot, Yasmeen left Jonathan and Amy at the entrance of the Art Institute and went into the restroom. They had spent the day touring the museum halls. Yasmeen lost herself in the exquisite paintings and fine sculptures.

On her way back from the restroom, a group of students in neat uniforms gathered with their teachers and blocked her path. She stepped to the side, approaching Jonathan and Amy from the back.

Jonathan had his hand on Amy's waist and his head bowed close to hers. They seemed involved in an intimate conversation. She stopped a decent distance away and waited, hating to intrude and interrupt their talk.

The students moved on and entered the building, taking their noisy energy with them.

Deciding if it was proper for her to join the others, she moved closer and heard Jonathan mention her name.

"Jasmine's so cold toward Adam. I just don't see the appeal for him."

Her steps faltered, and she came to a stop several steps behind the couple.

Amy pulled away from Jonathan. "I thought you liked her?"

"At first. Thought she might be the one to get him excited about life again. But after what I saw today, I'm not sure."

"What happened? Did I miss something? Adam looked like he was having a good time in the museum. Jasmine certainly enjoyed herself."

"Exactly my point. She studied the Goddamn paintings, he studied *her*. I wanted to shoot my brains out. She completely ignored him."

Her heartbeat quickening, she looked about her. This was wrong. She was eavesdropping. But she couldn't make herself move away.

"What is it with you men? If you're not the center of attention, then you're being ignored? There's a whole spectrum in between, you know. I thought the whole point of the trip was to distract her. She lost herself in the museum and maybe, just maybe, it got her mind off the horrible reality she's facing." Amy punched Jonathan's shoulder. "Did you think about that? Adam realized it and didn't interfere, caring and nice man that he is."

"What's that supposed to mean?"

"You're projecting your own views of a relationship to theirs, babe. Let them be. Adam's a grown man and doesn't need you to babysit him."

Her cheeks flaming, Yasmeen hid behind a big planter holding a tall shrub, and with shame, she continued to follow the conversation. Too late to join them now. They would know she heard their last comments.

"Are you sayin' I'm not carin' enough like Adam? Is that it? I'm not nice to you?"

"God! This's not about you. And let's face it, you're not one to give advice about marriage relationships."

"So that's where you're goin'? I thought we were talkin' about Adam and Jasmine."

"We are. I think you're adorable for wanting to protect your friend."

"Adam's too involved, and Jasmine cares nothin' for him."

"She comes from a totally different part of the world, babe. She's here in very unusual circumstances. To expect her to show her emotions like the rest of us isn't fair."

"Did she tell you anythin'? How she feels about him?"

Amy lifted her left hand and wiggled her fingers

in Jonathan's face. "She admires his sense of commitment."

Jonathan groaned.

Amy leaned over and kissed him. "Jasmine thinks Adam is a gentleman, a special man."

"That's a start, I guess."

Appalled with her actions, spying on her friends, Yasmeen slipped back into the building, making sure they didn't see her. When Adam stopped the truck by the curb, she hurried to go in, pretending she had just arrived. She sat mute, trying to absorb what she overheard. What was Jonathan talking about? What did he know about her feelings? Amy understood what it was like for her. Men were idiots, clueless to women emotional compositions. She glanced at Adam, driving in silence. Did he agree with his friend, that she was cold and uncaring?

Adam dropped off their friends at the hotel and continued on for dinner with her alone.

No. Not all men were idiots.

***

"Moroccan?" Yasmeen read the sign of the Middle Eastern restaurant, surprised at Adam's choice.

"Bad idea?" Adam hesitated before they entered.

"Great idea. I never had Moroccan food before."

They followed the hostess to the booth. Heavy burgundy curtains concealed a corner with a low table at the center. Numerous colorful cushions scattered on an intricately designed carpet instead of chairs. A mosaic glass and brass lantern centered the round table, and smaller matching lanterns dangled from the ceiling.

Yasmeen took off her shoes, placed them on a rack to the side, and sat on one of the cushions. She tucked her feet under the skirt of her dress.

Adam struggled to fit his long legs in the cramped space.

She pulled the table toward her to give him more room. "Just lean back on the wall and extend your leg toward the shoe rack."

"Don't want to be rude."

"Not rude at all. First time having a meal on the floor?"

"In a restaurant and in the company of a lady? Yup." He sat on the cushions, bent his knees, stretched them a couple of times before he settled in an awkward position.

A waiter wearing a long ivory robe and yellow

pointed slippers introduced their menus and provided recommendations when asked about the chef's favorite dishes. He took their orders and drew the curtains together concealing them in a tent-like setting. String instruments and drums played in the background. Somewhere above their heads, incense burned.

She smelled something familiar. Roses, almonds, pine wood? The smells of home. "I like this place. I can't wait to sink in."

Adam worked on rearranging the utensils on the table to place them at the proper angles for each setting. "Dig in." He pushed the lantern to the exact center of the table.

She put her hand on his to stop him. "Thank you."

"Just wanted you to learn the right expression. You sink your teeth into something when you're ang—"

"Thank you for a lovely day," she broke in. "The fantastic museum tour. This wonderful, almost magical place. I know what you are trying to do. It is working."

"I'm glad."

She folded her hands on the table and leaned over. "I know it has been difficult for you, the way I behaved the last couple of weeks. But I think I needed to go through that." She traced her fingers along the colorful designs cast by the lantern on the white tablecloth. "You can't undo a feeling, can you? You just have to let it run through until it stops being foreign, and you get used to it." She pulled back, resting her head on the wall. "No matter what the reasons may be, war rips through our lives. Some people die, some survive in one shape or form, and then there are people like me, hanging on the edge waiting for the end."

He opened his mouth to say something, but the waiter coughed from behind the curtain. "Excuse me, sir."

Adam parted the curtain and let the waiter in, balancing a big tray on top of his head.

Removing the table lantern to the floor, the waiter placed a round brass tray, the size of the table itself in front of them. He uncovered a clay pot and explained the rest of the dishes. As soon as he withdrew, Yasmeen held her spoon. "I'm digging in."

She guessed at some of the spices she tasted in the food, and Adam washed his mouth with water many times after each spicy bite. He kept the conversation light, telling her facts about Chicago and some of its history, throwing in a joke every now and then. Some she picked up on, and some she pretended to get to avoid hurting his feelings.

"Can I ask you something?"

"Ask away."

"What do the numbers of your computer password represent? Or are they random?"

He took long sips of water, shielding his face behind the tall glass.

Was he staling? She should not have asked, nosey and inconsiderate. Needing to feel closer to him, she didn't think on how inappropriate her question was. "I understand if you don't want to tell me. I didn't mean to pry into your private matters."

Draining his glass, he set it down. "It's the code Fadi sent me in his letter. The number that led me to you."

She picked up her drink and gulped, her mouth dry all of a sudden. His explanation, however, satisfied a different kind of thirst. One she paid attention to earlier in the day, growing stronger with every passing minute she spent in Adam's company.

"Thank you for telling me."

The meal progressed. Adam fidgeted in his seat many times, and she couldn't help feeling sorry for him, flattered by his efforts to conceal his obvious discomfort.

This was a sign of a caring man, her mother

would have whispered in her ear had she been here. But Mother wasn't here. She was far away, and *she* was alone with Adam, alone in an enchanted tent on a foreign land. How come she didn't feel panicked? Where did this serenity come from? Did he know what he was doing? Did he design this?

"I can't believe you dragged Jonathan through the art exhibits. Amy showed interest, but I think it was torture for him."

"He did it for you."

"Jonathan endured it because he cares about you, and I'm . . ."

Adam lifted his eyebrows prompting her to finish her sentence. "You're what?"

"I'm finding it hard not to."

The waiter showed up to take their tray away and replaced it with a tea and dessert tray.

Adam tapped his fingers on the table, impatient for the waiter to leave.

"Bring me the bill, please." He put his arms on the table and leaned closer to Yasmeen. There was no room for the slightest misunderstanding. He must find out what she meant by her statement. She would have to spell it out for him, damn it.

"What're you saying?"

She stirred sugar cubes in a tall glass stuffed

with mint leaves. "I'm tired of waiting for an end. I want to make my own start."

His cell phone rang from his pants pocket. Stretching and twisting to one side, he took out the phone after it went silent. He glanced at the screen and tossed it aside on one of the cushions. "Sorry! Unknown number again."

Her eyes fixed on the twirling mint leaves, her cheeks turned red.

"Yasmeen?"

She didn't respond.

He placed his index finger under her chin and lifted it. "What's wrong?"

"Is it time to leave?"

"Soon as I pay the bill." He retrieved his hand, perplexed at her transformation, the sudden shift of her mood. What did he miss?

"Are we meeting Amy and Jonathan tonight?" Yasmeen's voice was low, subdued.

"We can try to call their room when we get back to the hotel." He grabbed his cell phone. "I'll call Amy on her cell right now, if you'd like."

Yasmeen entwined her fingers on the table, her knuckles turning white. "Don't. There is no need to disturb them."

"Is something bothering you?"

"Are we staying in the same room?"

The waiter coughed from behind the curtain. Damn it, not now. Adam pulled the curtain aside and snatched the bill. He waited for him to walk away. "I booked two rooms. Don't want you to feel obliged in any way to have to share . . . a room with me. I want you to be comfortable."

She nodded once. "Thank you."

He paid, ushered a distant and quiet Yasmeen out of the restaurant. He stopped at a gas station on the way to fill the almost empty tank. Before he left the truck, he turned to Yasmeen. "Need anything from the store?"

She shook her head.

He pondered his situation while he waited for the gas pump to stop. Why did she shut down all of a sudden? He glanced at her from behind the window. She had her head turned toward the store. What did she mean by making her own start? The pump's valve clicked. He went into the store to pay, keeping his eyes on the truck the whole time.

Bright neon lights illuminated the storefront entire glass wall. A wiry old man entered the store behind Adam. Something about the way he moved grabbed Yasmeen's attention. The man zeroed in on Adam like a hawk stalking his prey. The man hid behind one of the coolers, clearly trying to conceal himself, cocking his head sideways every now and then, watching Adam. She had seen that sort of behavior before. Surveillance men in plain clothes stood out on the streets at home no matter how hard they tried to blend in. This man looked familiar, the way he squared his shoulders while he walked. If only she could take a closer look at his face.

Adam left the store and headed her way. The man followed him outside and got in a white van parked by the side of the store. When Adam drove the truck onto the street, she lost her view of the van and the man, putting him out of her mind.

***

Adam showed Yasmeen how to use the key card to open the hotel room and handed it over. He walked in ahead of her, switched the main light, placed her small travel bag on the stand, and checked the room. He pointed to the right. "I'll be next door. If you need anything, just let me know."

Yasmeen stayed by the window, her hands clasped behind her back.

He hooked his thumbs in his jeans back pockets. "You tired?"

She nodded.

He walked out to the hallway. "Get a good

night's sleep. We've a lot to see tomorrow." He tried to smile but his insides were in a knot. Damn it, what did he do wrong? He went into his room, threw his backpack on the bed, and stared out the window. He did the right thing, didn't he? The ball was in her court now.

He turned on the TV and went into the bathroom. He lowered his head under the cold running water trying to drown out Jonathan's voice in his head. *You're a fool, Adam Wegener.*

Stretching on the bed, his body ached in many ways. The circulation in his left leg suffered from the awkward position on the floor during dinner. He contemplated walking over to Yasmeen's room, asking her to massage it with those magic fingers of hers. Forget it. His chest constricted, wanting something more than air. His hands missed the silky feel of her hair. He used the remote control to flip between the channels on TV, not really watching anything.

A knock sounded on his door. He lifted his head and muted the volume. She came to him. He jumped off the bed and almost ripped the door off its hinges.

A wiry old man leaned against the jamb, with his hands in his pockets. "Hello, son."

CHAPTER 20

A PEEK

Adam stared at an older version of himself. He staggered back. The knot in his stomach dropped to his knees. His mind froze. He squinted for better focus.

"That the way to greet your old man?" Fred Shipman pushed past him into the room and shoved his shoulder on the way. "I know you're in shock, son. No need to be rude."

Adam kept the door open with one hand. His eyes flew to the closet door searching for a hideout like he had done so often as a child.

"What the hell are you doing here?"

"Bet you thought I dropped outa the face of the earth, didn't you?" Fred plopped on the sofa, stretched his arms to the sides. "Been keepin' track of you for a while."

"How did you know I was here?"

"Followed you from the gas station." Fred crossed his ankles on the coffee table. "You were too busy eyein' that little number you had in your truck, you didn't see me."

Adam's shock turned to panic. If Yasmeen opened her door she would walk into this nightmare. He closed the door and advanced toward his father. "That's my wife," he kept his tone menacing. He hoped Fred heard the threat in his voice.

Fred lifted his head sideways. A slow smile parted his lips. "Good for you. Where's she? I wanna meet my daughter-in-law."

"The hell you will," Adam spat. "You're going to forget you ever saw her."

Fred held his hands up. "Hold on, son. I'm not here to mess with you."

Adam bent down and put his hands on the back of the sofa by Fred's head. He brought his face close and smelled cigarettes and alcohol on the man's breath. His stomach lurched.

"Don't . . . call me . . . son."

"You're still bitter. Fifteen years've passed and you haven't changed."

"There's been no reason to change." The muscles in his arms quivered. He brought his face even closer, forcing Fred to tilt his head back. "Have you changed?"

"Actually, I have."

He drew back and looked down at his father.

"Did you have a heart transplant or something? A leopard can't shed its spots."

Fred lowered his feet to the floor and scooted forward. "Tried to call you. You hung up on me. Told me not to call again."

"I don't see the point."

"I have a family now. A good wife and two daughters."

"You had a family," he shouted. "And a good wife." He had better get a grip, not let Fred provoke him further.

Fred jumped up to get in Adam's face. "You kicked me outa my own home. Kept me away from my family all those years."

"I was fifteen, you selfish son-of-a-bitch. I had to protect my mother from the monster you were. Had to drag her out from the bottom of the lake."

Fred held his shoulders. "I was a different person."

Adam flinched and pulled back.

"Look, I didn't come here to talk about the past. I forgive you."

"*You* forgive *me*?"

"I'm tellin' you, I've been blessed." A spark danced in the old man's eyes. "I found God, and He's led me to a new life. He's tellin' me it's time to connect with you again, to give you another chance."

Adam thumped his chest. "Give *me* another chance?" He unbuttoned his shirt. "When God granted you this new life, did He make you forget a few things?" He pointed at the scar under his collarbone. "Because He sure as hell didn't erase anything from my memory."

Fred looked away. "You gotta let go of the past. It's the only way to move forward."

Adam let out an anguished cry. He took hold of Fred's arms. "Damn you. Look at my fucking scar."

"There's not much of a scar. It doesn't look like anythin' more than animal scratches."

"You're the goddamn animal who did this." He shoved Fred back against the wall. "You heated that screwdriver and branded me in the same spot every fucking time. These aren't scratches, you sadistic fuck." He grabbed fistfuls of Fred's shirt and slammed his back on the wall with each word he uttered. "These are a hundred and thirty-six torturous, searing, festering wounds."

"You counted them?" Fred curled his lips in a sneer.

"You were always one to exaggerate an issue."

"I counted, alright." He let him go and stepped back, repulsed. "You know how long it takes for burns like that to heal?" He flexed his hands to stop them from shaking. "An eternity. A damned eternity."

Fred stumbled forward and tripped on the coffee table. He managed to maintain his balance. "You can blame me all you want, but at the end of the day, you are who you are. My son, no matter what name you chose to live your life by." He overlapped his hands on his chest and exhaled. "Unlike you, I have a good life now. I'm truly happy."

"You know nothing about my life, you delusional selfish prick." He took measured steps toward the door, looked through the peep hole to make sure Yasmeen wasn't there. Putting his hand on the door handle, he turned around. "Get out of here. Crawl back into whatever hole you came out of. You can be happy there, away from me." He opened the door and nodded for Fred to leave.

Fred pulled out a piece of paper from his pocket and dropped it on the coffee table. "Your mother didn't do you any favors passin' on her delicate nature. You were always too timid as a boy. Tried to toughen you up. Turn you into a man. My contact numbers're here." He sauntered to the door. "Call me when you stop cryin' and grow some balls."

Adam slammed the door. The vibrations were certain to wake up everyone in the hallway. He put his palms together, pressed his thumbs on his lips, and paced the room. His anger mushroomed by the second. Fred's smoky repugnant scent permeated the room. How did viciousness have its own distinctive odor?

The sofa's white cushions were still indented from Fred's weight. Adam fluffed them back to their original shape. He went into the bathroom, pulled a couple of tissues and returned to the coffee table. He wiped off the marks left behind by Fred's shoes. "Shit, I need to get out of here." He buttoned his shirt, grabbed his key card and opened the door.

Yasmeen stood in the hallway with her fist raised to the door and a disturbed look on her face. "I heard a lot of shouting. Are you fighting with Jonathan?" She craned her neck to look past him into the room. "Is Amy alright?"

Crap. This couldn't be happening. "I had the TV too loud, sorry."

"Where are you going?"

"To the reception desk. There's something I need to take care of."

Yasmeen frowned. "Your shirt is not buttoned right."

She undid the mismatched buttons.

Adam stood still, bewildered, while she worked on his shirt. Now? Of all times? When he couldn't form a coherent thought in his head? When his anger was raw enough to crush someone? He watched her hands move, taunting him. If he weren't on the verge of completely losing control, he would lay his hands on her, caress her neck and feel that creamy skin of hers under his fingertips. He clenched his jaw instead and waited for her to be done.

"There." Yasmeen dropped her hands. "That looks better."

He stepped out and closed the door behind him. "Thanks. See you for breakfast at eight?"

Yasmeen nodded, her hair spilled over her shoulders, releasing fragrant flowers in the air around him.

He held his breath. She had better go inside, before he lost it.

She lifted her eyelashes and examined his face. "You are angry," her voice soft, unsure.

He hid his shaking hands in his pockets. "Good night."

She flinched, stepped back and went into her room.

Great job! Scaring her with his rough response, coming out like a threat rather than a wish for a pleasant night. He hurried to the elevators, hoping to God there would be some drunk at the hotel bar he could pick a fight with and end this miserable night.

***

Adam scraped the bottom of the lake, his hands frantically searching for something. His lungs hurt and his ears rang with pain. His right hand connected with something soft, he closed his fingers around it, and kicked as hard as he could to swim upward. His head broke the surface. He opened his mouth and gulped for air.

He lay flat on his back on the bed in his hotel room, drenched in sweat. His right hand clutched a jumbled sheet. The ringing phone pounded nails into his head. He turned on his side, snatched the phone handset and put it over his ear. The wake-up call recorded message declared the time as 7:00 a.m. He dropped the handset back. Swinging his legs to the floor, he held his head in his hands. The simple movement nauseated him. What the hell did he do last night?

He shuffled to the bathroom. His eyes beheld a strange face in the mirror. Haggard and washed out. A man appearing years older in a strange twisted way. And his hands hurt. Dried blood caked on his knuckles. Did he fight with someone? He examined his face, then his chest through his torn shirt. There were few fresh marks on him. An image of Yasmeen unbuttoning his shirt flashed through his head. Oh, God! What did he do?

He stumbled out of the bathroom and dialed Yasmeen's room number. The contents of his stomach jumped to his throat a couple of times. She answered after the fourth ring.

"You alright?"

"Um . . . good morning?"

"Morning," he rushed. "Are you okay?"

"I'm fine, why? We agreed on eight, right?" her voice soft, gentle, and soothing.

"Right. Just making sure you're up." Dear God, thank you. "See you in a bit." He hung up, dropped on the bed, and flexed his bruised hands.

CHAPTER 21

A BLAZE

Yasmeen took one last look in the mirror, draped her jacket on one arm, and answered the door. "Amy?"

"The men are already downstairs drinking coffee. You ready?"

Checking her watch, she walked out. "Am I late?"

"Right on time. Adam called and asked me to come fetch you before I headed to the restaurant. He needed to talk to Jonathan in private, I guess." Amy nudged her shoulder with hers as they headed to the elevators. "This's our chance to have some girl talk." She tilted her head. "Anything you'd like to tell me?"

"Do you know what we are doing today?"

"I want to go shopping at some point before we head out." Amy chatted about what she wanted to buy until they reached the men's table.

Adam slumped in one corner, his hands in his lap, talking to Jonathan. He wore sunglasses.

Yasmeen's steps faltered. Odd. Why would he wear sunglasses inside the restaurant? He barely moved and stopped talking when she approached. What was wrong with him?

A waitress placed plates piled with pancakes on the table as soon as she and Amy took their seats.

"I took the liberty orderin' for everyone." Jonathan stuck his fork in a stack of fluffy pancakes and transferred them to his plate.

"Thanks, babe, I'm starving." Amy dumped butter and syrup on her pile.

Adam refilled his cup from the coffee thermos on the table, his knuckles red and scraped.

She scooted closer. "Are you sick?"

Jonathan waved his fork in Adam's direction. "He's hung over. He'll be fine once he takes in enough water." He refilled Adam's glass.

She had no idea what Jonathan meant. She looked at Amy for guidance, but the woman had her eyes on her food. She felt Adam's hand on hers.

"Repercussions of drinking too much last night. It'll pass."

"Shit-faced is what I'd call it," Jonathan mumbled with his mouth full. Syrup oozed from one side.

"You told me you don't drink alcohol."

"Stopped a long time ago. Last night, something

happened. I . . . slipped."

"Mister Fred Shipman paid him a visit," Jonathan announced to the whole restaurant.

Amy gasped. "You're kidding. Last night? Here in this hotel?"

Adam rubbed his forehead. "For the love of God, keep it down."

"Fred's been followin' him," Jonathan continued in the same tone.

Withdrawing her hand from under Adam's, she sucked in a long breath. "You hit your father?"

"What? No. I had a fight with a punk at the bar, that's all. Can we drop it now? I don't want it to ruin our day."

She tried to eat a few bites. Her mind worked overtime, replaying last night's events, connecting the dots. The shouts, Adam's disheveled appearance, his abruptness. She thought of the call he made this morning, the urgency in his voice when he asked if she was alright. Did he suspect he hurt her too? She picked at her food. Amy and Jonathan faded into the background of her mind. Her senses tuned to a brooding Adam next to her. She slipped her hand under the table and entwined her fingers with his.

White snow blanketed the ground and reflected

the cold day's bright sun into Yasmeen's eyes. Leaving the men behind, she went on a shopping spree with Amy, bought sunglasses and felt silly wearing them in the dead of winter. She also bought a couple of shirts for Adam, choosing colors and styles she preferred to see on him. If he let her.

Adam and Jonathan joined them for lunch at a pizzeria near the hotel. Adam looked better. Normal color returned to his face. "You might want to change into pants for the afternoon."

"Why? What is wrong with my skirt? Where are we going?"

"Trust me, you want to be wearing pants." Adam ran his eyes over her. "And a thick turtleneck."

"And long socks," Amy added.

"You are not going to tell me, are you?"

"Nope." Adam left the table. "Come on, I'll walk back with you. Need to pack and check out before we head there."

***

Yasmeen held on to Adam's arm with both hands for dear life at the edge of the Millennium Park Ice Skating Rink. Her legs stiffened, refusing to slide her skates on the ice. Her nose ran, but she couldn't risk letting go to wipe it. People skated in front of her with ease. Those who fell to the ice laughed and got up again. In time, she felt more embarrassed than scared and enjoyed watching the bodies twirl to the background music.

"No need to rush. Take your time." Adam patted her arm. "But if we don't move soon, we'll freeze."

Amy and Jonathan skidded to a stop in front of them. Amy tugged at Yasmeen's elbow. "Just try. Come on, I'll hold one hand, Adam the other. You don't have to do anything, we'll drag you."

"Don't let me fall." If little children could do it, she could.

Jonathan stood behind them, put his hands on her waist and gave her a gentle shove to get her started. They moved, she screamed, and by some graceful power, she stayed on her feet. They skated two full circles on the outer perimeter of the rink, the cold wind blowing in her face, invigorating her. She gained more confidence by the minute.

A teenager whizzed by Amy. She had to turn to avoid crashing into him. The movement unbalanced Yasmeen, and she yanked Adam's hand, tilting him sideways. He tried to maintain his balance, but it seemed the muscles in his left leg were too weak to hold him upright in that awkward angle. He crashed to the ground, pulling her and Amy down with him.

Jonathan arrived a couple of seconds later and managed to stay clear of the pile up. He laughed down at them.

"Don't just stand there, babe." Amy reached up. "Give us a hand."

They untangled their bodies. Jonathan helped Yasmeen get to a bench outside the rink, Adam limped behind.

"I'm going to find that kid and beat the crap out of him," Amy skated away Jonathan hurried back to her side.

"That was fun." Yasmeen held the back of the bench with both hands and dropped her body down.

"You okay? You didn't hit your head or anything?" Adam hobbled to sit next to her.

"I think I landed on you, mostly." She laughed and rubbed her right elbow. "You?"

"Don't think I can get back on the ice again." He clutched his leg. "Sorry, usually I last longer than a couple of rounds."

"You would have if it weren't for me. Did you bring your pills with you?"

"Don't need them for this." He stood and stomped his feet, careful to hold on to the bench. "I'll get my shoes. Do you want to try again? Shall I call them and give that poor kid a break?"

"Oh, no. I'm done. Can you bring my boots?"

She pointed at her feet. "I'm not going to try to walk in these."

Adam took off his gloves, went down to one knee in front of her, extending his left leg to the side. "I'll return them." He unlaced her skates, his hands working fast.

She touched his shoulders. "I can do this myself. Please don't strain your leg further."

His hands stopped moving. "It's okay. I know someone with magic fingers who can massage it and make it all better." He looked up at her with a grin on his face.

She stiffened. "That one time I tried didn't end well, remember?"

He released a ragged breath. "I remember." He pulled one skate off. "Relax. Didn't mean anything by it." He worked on the other skate and then moved to sit on the bench. "It was a joke. Never mind."

"Please don't get angry. I don't understand what you mean half the time."

He placed the pair of skates on the ground. "It's frustrating, that's all. I don't get some of the stuff you say, either."

"Really? I'm sorry. Like what?"

He produced a couple of tissues from his pocket, handed her one and used the other to wipe his hands. "I was thinking about what you said at dinner last night. That you want to make your own start? What did you mean?"

She stared ahead at the mingling crowds, children nestled in family circles, couples glued to each other, laughing, snapping pictures and sharing memorable moments. A boy, not older than four, wobbled on his skates toward the rink in front of them. A woman rushed after him, yelling at him to slow down.

"I want to have a normal life, to feel like I belong here."

Adam caressed her cheek with the back of his fingers. "You do."

She lifted her feet up on the bench, hugged her knees to her chest and covered her feet with the fringe of her wool scarf. "Will you tell me what happened with your father last night?"

"I'd rather not get into that." His voice fell flat, and his hands hid in his pockets. "It was a disaster."

She waited for him to add more, but he stared in the distance and remained quiet, the pain on his face undeniable. Was he trying to shield her from the ugliness? Did he think her that fragile? Or was it a trust issue? If he thought her uncaring like Jonathan had said, he wouldn't open up to her about something so hurtful and private. She should find a way to encourage him, show him she understood. But how? What could she do? Resting her chin on her raised knees, she tucked on the scarf around her sock-clad feet. "Perhaps you will tell me in good time?"

"Yeah. In good time." He balanced on his skates. "You're cold. I'll get our shoes."

Adam headed to the rental station, bought steaming hot chocolate from one of the stands and walked back, careful to keep her boots tucked under his arm. Passing through a big crowd gathered at the main entrance, he saw the back of a man standing next to Yasmeen. He shouldn't have left her alone. Some jerk was talking to her and she didn't have shoes to walk away. He moved faster. The man gestured at the empty space next to Yasmeen on the bench. She nodded, and he sat down. His face came into full view.

Adam's pulse quickened. The cups in his hands splashed hot liquid on his fingers. He dropped the drinks in a trash bin, hurrying ahead. A few steps away, he saw Yasmeen scoot to one end of the bench, her head moved scanning the crowds. She was searching for him. Her face relaxed the instant her eyes connected with his. Out of breath, he made it to her side, handed her the boots, and ran one hand on her head down to her shoulder, giving it a gentle squeeze. "Sorry it took so long."

"I had the pleasure of introducin' myself to your lovely wife." Fred's eyes mocked him.

He ambled to Fred's side and grabbed his arm. "Let's talk."

Fred rose. "No need to get testy."

"Thought I made myself clear last night," Adam stressed every word.

"Saw this as my chance to meet your wife, since you weren't gonna introduce me any time soon." A sly smile transformed Fred's face. "Was about to ask if she knows how to swim."

He yanked Fred's arm. "Get the hell out of here."

Fred turned to Yasmeen. "Come visit sometime. You're family now." He pulled away from Adam's grip and walked off.

Adam followed him with his eyes. Taking deep breaths, he turned back to Yasmeen. She was shaking.

"You okay?"

Yasmeen threw her arms around his neck. "You may look like your father, but you are nothing like him."

Adam held her tight, buried his face in her hair.

"Why did you say that?"

Yasmeen tried to pull her head back, but she only managed to slide her cheek across his. "Because it is true," she whispered.

He sealed his lips to hers, appalled by his roughness. He couldn't have moved with more finesse if he tried. Like pulling the trigger of a rifle, her embrace released something urgent inside him, and he crushed her closer, giving thanks to the words she uttered.

Yasmeen brought her hands down to his chest and pushed.

God Almighty, was he hurting her again? He withdrew his head and kept her in his arms. She stopped pushing. Condensation from their mingling breaths swirled in the small space between them. He examined her face. She had her eyes cast down to his throat, her cheeks scarlet red. "Look at me," his voice full of emotions he didn't want to conceal.

She shook her head and whispered, "I can't."

"Am I that repulsive to you?"

"How could you think that?"

"Then allow me to do it right." He brought his face down and took his time introducing her to a proper kiss. Thinking himself the teacher, she the hesitant pupil, his heart swelled in his chest, taken by surprise. He was the eager student, acquiring a taste for the unknown, his senses saturated by her feminine allure, discovering where he belonged.

Yasmeen's body lost its tension, and he felt her lean into him, showing him acceptance, reserved and uncertain as it may be. Her hands inched up to his nape and her fingers pulled on his hair.

He deepened the kiss. This was it. This was his place.

Several heartbeats later, the sounds of the world around them pushed through the fog in his head. Jonathan's voice in the distance announced it was time to hit the road and head home for Platteville.

CHAPTER 22

A HURRICANE

Yasmeen took the front seat as Adam drove Jonathan's truck on the way back. They left later than planned, which put them on the highway well after dark. Jonathan and Amy slumped in the backseat, asleep.

Yasmeen remained wide-awake, reflecting on her time with Adam the last couple of days, especially the last few hours. What happened back there by the ice rink? Her first kiss, strange and comforting at the same time, she had nothing to compare it to. Adam's reaction to her words took her by surprise. She should not have said it, though. She did not want to be another wedge between father and son, no matter what kind of history they had. But the words flew out of her mouth when she saw the two men side-by-side. She stole a quick look at Adam, both hands on the wheel, his eyes focused on the road. Did he know the chaos he created inside her?

Turning her face to the side, she stared outside

her window. The world she knew fell into decay, most of her family and friends dead or missing. Did the survivors know she thought about them? Did the dead know they would not be forgotten? Their faces not just sketched in her notebook, but also engraved in her head?

Here she was in the middle of this vast frozen land, thinking of the possibility of a future with the man beside her. What kind of person did that make her? What would she do with this unfamiliar longing his kiss generated? She ran her fingertips over her lips. Maybe that was what she needed, an intimate moment that shook her core, a hurricane to wipe her earth clean, sprout a new world and a new Yasmeen.

She laid her head back and closed her eyes. Fred's long thin face stared at her, eyes as cold and hard as the ice she fell on. His words were nice enough, but it was the way he said them, the voice he used that clawed her insides. It reminded her of another foul sound, one she listened to every morning on her way to school for ten years. The *Mukhabarat* guards next to her house spoke nice words as she passed by, but she also heard the sound of venom drip from their mouths and hit the ground. Adam's kind voice couldn't be more different.

"Say something."

"Are you alright?"

"I'm fine. Why?"

"You've been very quiet."

His voice soothed her, massaged her soul. Keep talking, Adam. She opened her eyes and turned her head to look at him. "I told you before. I'm not as fragile as you think."

He checked the rear-view mirror. "Are they really asleep?"

She twisted in her seat to check. Amy's head nestled on Jonathan's lap. His head leaned on the window, his mouth hung open. "It appears so."

"Listen, I know an encounter with Fred can be very . . . disturbing. I'm afraid my actions only added to your confusion. Sorry you had to be involved in his monkey business."

"Is that what he does? Works with monkeys? In a zoo?"

Adam cleared his throat. "I meant his manipulative tactics, dirty work—"

"Okay, I understand now. And you don't need to apologize for him."

"What did he say to you before I got there?"

"Not much. He told me who he was and asked where I was from originally. He said I looked ex . . . ex something. He used an unfamiliar word."

Adam's knuckles on the wheel turned white. "Did you tell him?"

"I didn't open my mouth. Can you imagine if he heard me talk? He would definitely know I'm not from here and ask more questions." She searched for a way to lighten the mood and put his mind at ease. "He was polite."

Adam flinched. A muscle in his jaw jerked. He dropped his right hand to the seat by his side and balled it into a fist. "I know exactly how polite he can be."

She placed her hand over his. "Can we stop at a gas station or something? I really need to use the restroom."

"There's a McDonald's coming up in about ten minutes." He rubbed his thumb over her hand. "Can you hold it until then?"

"We will see. Just don't make me laugh."

"How far is the next stop?" Jonathan gripped the back of her seat. "I need to pee."

Yasmeen burst out laughing and Adam pushed the gas pedal.

***

Blowing into his coffee cup, Adam waited for the ladies to come out of the restroom. "We'll probably be home around eleven," he told Jonathan who was busy unwrapping a sandwich. "I start another shift tomorrow." He took a sip and winced. "Not looking forward to that."

"Why do you do that to yourself?" Jonathan bit into his sandwich. "You have hired hands to do it as part of their jobs. You don't have to shovel manure all week."

"Have to share the load. The Abeldeens work too hard, and I can't afford another hand."

"Bein' married is costly, huh?" Jonathan looked dejected. "If you need anythin', I got your back."

"Save your money, my friend. Have a feeling you'll need every penny. For some reason beyond my comprehension, Amy wants to be your wife."

"Don't I know it."

Adam lifted an eyebrow. "So, what're you waiting for?"

"Courage, I guess."

"What's taking them so long?" Adam looked at his watch. "What're they doing in there?"

Jonathan threw the wrapping of his sandwich in the trash bin. "You're in a hurry to get home, for someone who's not lookin' forward to spend tomorrow buried in shit."

"What's that supposed to mean?"

"I saw what I saw back there by the ice rink.

Jasmine's softened toward you, hasn't she?" He slapped Adam on the back. "Told you this trip was a good idea."

Adam swung his coffee cup to the side to avoid a spill. "You saw Fred talk to her?"

"Yeah. We were on the far side of the rink. From the looks of it, she handled him well. And you, my friend, handled her even better."

Adam couldn't stop from smiling and remained quiet.

"You do see the irony in this, don't you?"

"What irony?"

"Your father brought you closer to your wife. You should be thankful for him showin' up like that after all these years."

CHAPTER 23

A TRUTH

Adam entered the dark kitchen in the early morning hours. The clock struck four. He poured a cup of coffee and stood by the window, dreading the day ahead. A quiet snow fell through the night and into the morning, but he barely slept the night before, aware that he broke one barrier between himself and Yasmeen.

Jonathan's remarks about Fred's recent role in his life played havoc with his nerves and kept him tossing in his bed. Did Yasmeen show him signs of acceptance because of a different type of emotion? Sympathy? Pity? Should he have followed up on that kiss last night? Would she have welcomed him because she felt sorry for him, nothing more? Damn you Fred, if that were true.

Moving to the sink to wash his cup, he bumped his foot on something. He switched on the lights. It was the footstool Yasmeen had bought for Sara to use when she came for art lessons. Kicking it aside, his eyes landed on the big manila envelope in the center of the table. Sam's envelope.

He examined the stack of papers. Yasmeen's signature was scribbled on the indicated lines of the residency application. He sank into a chair. When did she sign them? Last night after he went to bed? Contemplating waking her, he checked the time. Too early. He put the papers back inside the envelope, rolled it to fit in his jacket pocket and walked out. He'd mail it as soon as the post office opened.

Late afternoon, Adam slumped on his horse, exhausted and sick to his stomach with his stench. He looked forward to a hot shower and clean clothes. Trotting into the barn, he removed the saddle and was preparing Earnest for the night when he heard Yasmeen come in. He stepped behind the horse, crusted manure stuck to his work pants and boots.

"Don't come closer," he yelled out.

"There is a man on the phone for you."

"Take his name. Tell him I'll call back in fifteen minutes."

"He insisted, Adam. Said it is urgent. His name is Scott."

He stepped around Earnest and strode toward Yasmeen. Big Scott always emailed, never called.

Yasmeen put her hand over her nose and mouth

and handed him the phone. He turned his back. "Hey, Scott."

"Listen, Fadi's going to call you in ten minutes."

He checked his watch. "Where is he?"

"He won't tell me. He's using a reporter's phone. Said he tried to call your cell a number of times, but never got through. I gave him your home number."

"Did he tell you anything specific?"

"No. I checked the list of pardoned prisoners the Syrians released today. His father's name isn't on it."

He attempted to move further into the barn away from Yasmeen to spare her his horrible stink, but the phone almost went out of range. He retreated his steps to stay rooted in front of her. "Anything else I should know?"

"That's all I have. Keep it short just in case."

He shoved the phone into Yasmeen's free hand. "Fadi will call in a few minutes."

Her eyes widened. "Fadi? Call here?"

"Go back inside and wait for the call." He took off his boots and started to unzip his pants. "I'll be there in a minute. Now go."

Yasmeen ran back to the house.

Discarding his work clothes, he washed with the

barn hose as fast as he could, put on a clean outfit, ran to the house, and yanked the door open.

Yasmeen stood by the fridge talking on the phone.

He went to the sink and scrubbed his hands and face again with soap and warm water. He watched her, reading clues in her voice and body language.

She spoke in Arabic and repeated one word many times, *"Hader."*

He'd heard Iraqi soldiers say that word when they took orders from their senior officers. He assumed it denoted compliance. Was she being instructed?

Yasmeen extended the phone to Adam, her hand shaking. "Fadi wants to talk to you. He doesn't have a lot of time."

He put the receiver to his ear. "Fadi?"

"I don't know when I will be able to call again so listen carefully."

"Listening."

"I appreciate all you have done for my sister. There is no way Yasmeen can return to Syria. I told her it's safer to join our mother in Jordan if she wants to. They will be well protected there. Scott has the information to make the arrangements if she decides to go."

"Anything I can do for you?"

"I didn't tell her about our father. Please break it to her gently."

Fadi's voice disappeared, the background noise of shouts and distant explosions too loud for Adam to ignore. "The possibility of him being alive is slim," Fadi yelled over the din. "I'm running out of time myself. They are bound to catch me."

"Can you get out? To Turkey again?"

"I'm screwed. Please make sure she's taken care of."

The line went dead.

Adam placed the phone handset on the table, his stomach twisted into knots.

Yasmeen's eyes were fixed on him. "How bad is it? For Fadi?"

He stepped closer, wondering how to soften the news. "If he finds a way out of Syria, Scott will help him get to safety."

"Fadi will never leave home. He insists on doing his part to the end." She grasped the edge of the kitchen counter. "They will go after everyone if no one stops them. It happened before, but the world didn't see it." She hung her head. "Father talked about it all the time while I was growing up. He told me those innocent civilians should be remembered, no one deserves to disappear like that. Fadi knows he must do everything he can to prevent it from happening again." She snapped her head up. "I can't go home anymore, can I?"

"You have a home here."

Yasmeen blinked tears away. "Mother is safe in Jordan, right? Fadi said you will tell me why Father is not with her."

He inched closer and turned her toward him. "Yasmeen, your father was arrested before he made it across the border."

She crossed her arms. "That is not true. Why are you lying?"

He rubbed his hands up and down her arms. "Wish I was."

"I don't believe you."

"It's the truth. I'm sorry." He wrapped his arms around her, keeping her from pulling away.

She beat on his chest with her fists, her eyes wild and panicked. "How do you know?"

"Fadi told me when I saw him in Istanbul. He didn't know how to break it to you."

Her Face froze and she stopped struggling. "Do you know what that means?"

He tightened his hold and waited for her shock to give way to acceptance.

She let out an anguished cry. "The things they are doing to him?!"

If it hadn't been for his support, she would have

collapsed to the ground. Gently lowering her to the floor, he cradled her on his legs and leaned his back on the cabinet under the sink.

Yasmeen bent sideways, retching. She vomited over his knee.

He held her hair, and when she stopped convulsing, he pushed her head back to rest on his shoulder.

He listened to Yasmeen weep until the setting sun turned the kitchen dark. The noise of the fridge's motor droned in the background. Outside, a cat jumped on the windowsill and begged for attention. Vomit seeped under his thigh. His back hurt and his leg stiffened. How could he stop the visions that would flood Yasmeen's thoughts?

"Fadi's working on his release," Adam lied. He knocked the back of his head on the cabinet door. What was the point in hiding the truth? His entire life, he tried to stay honest as much as possible. But if it eased Yasmeen's pain, he would lie again and again. "Today, the government issued pardons for some political prisoners because of international pressure. They may do it again. It's possible he'll be out soon."

Yasmeen pulled away from him, crawled to the table, and used it for support to stand. "It will not be soon enough." Her voice sounded scratched and weak. "My father is better off dead."

CHAPTER 24

A DECISION

Adam braced himself for another round of grief. This one would be more profound, more heart wrenching. Yasmeen disappeared into her room for the rest of the evening. She asked him to go away when he checked on her.

He ate alone in the kitchen, his mind racing for ways to help her, and salvage the progress he'd made in their relationship. He was encouraged by the fact that she signed the papers before she knew she couldn't go back. It seemed like a decision she made, not something she did for lack of options. Now she had the option to join her mother, would she change her mind?

Drained and disconnected, he remembered the months he endured after he returned home from Iraq. Calm winds settled his sails after the storm, beauty painted the world around him, and life bloomed with possibilities. Still, he struggled to accept his new realities, suffering the mundane day-to-day normalcy as if he was put on hold, waiting for someone to resume the call. He waited for the period at the end of his line and for the start that never came. It had to come down to this woman, who didn't understand him when he spoke most of the time, to tap that button and reconnect him to his life. She won't go anywhere, not if he could help it.

He cleared the table, turned off the lights, and went upstairs, needing a hot shower and a couple of pills to sleep. Stopping in front of Yasmeen's door, he leaned his head on the wood and listened for sounds of her crying. Nothing. Leaving the bathroom with a towel wrapped around his waist, another draped around his neck, he walked barefoot to his room and stumbled to an abrupt stop.

Yasmeen stood by his window, hands clasped behind her back. She wore a black robe with a lavender satin bow under her chin. A lavender nightgown peeked from the slightly parted front.

"Can we talk?" Her gaze was steady, but he sensed a tremor in her voice.

"Sure."

"I will wait until you get dressed."

He waited for her to turn her head away, avert her eyes, but she didn't. He gave her his back, took the towel off his shoulders and opened his closet door.

"Who is Bradley Andrews?"

Reaching for his pants, his hand froze mid-air. The tattoo on his back. He stepped into the pants, threw aside the towel, and turned to face her.

She had not moved. Her face lost all color.

"That's Bradley *and* Andrews. There's an ampersand in the middle." He drew the logogram in the air. "You know, it's like an *and* sign."

Yasmeen's eyebrows knitted together. "Can you turn around, please? Let me see it again."

He faced the closet. She moved closer. Her breath brushed his damp skin.

"So, who are they?"

"Soldiers in my team. We were in the same . . ." His breath caught in his chest when he felt her finger trace the entwined letters at the top of his shoulder. "Same platoon in Iraq."

"Why are their names tattooed on your shoulder?" Her finger snaked its way down the letters to the middle of his back.

"We were caught in the same explosion. They were behind me. I survived, they didn't." He closed his eyes and prayed for her curiosity to end.

"They landed on your back?"

He spun around, knocking her hand out of the way. "Parts of them. Mostly flesh and some bones. They were blown to pieces." He grabbed her elbow with more force than he intended. "Why are you here? Why is this important for you to know?"

"Fadi said your friend has the contact information for my mother. Can I call her?"

He let go of her arm. "Of course. Big Scott said he'd email me the info. I checked. He hasn't yet." He snatched a tee-shirt from the closet and slipped it on. Why the change in subject? Shit, he scared her. Again, Damn it.

"Did you see the papers I left on the table this morning?"

"Mailed them already. Meant to talk to you about it at dinner, but the call . . ."

Yasmeen folded her arms around her and nodded. "Good. I don't want for you to get in legal trouble."

"You're not going to get me in any." He stretched his tee-shirt over his pants, needing to keep his hands busy. So that's why she signed them?

"If I ask you something, will you answer me honestly?" Yasmeen twisted the satin ribbon dangling from the bow on her chest.

He concentrated on keeping his eyes on her face, and not on the bow that started to get undone. "Always."

"Do you regret getting . . . involved?" Tears spilled down her cheeks. "I must know before I talk to my mother."

He held her face between his palms and wiped her tears with his thumbs. "I regret not doing more."

CHAPTER 25

FORGOTTEN

Yasmeen shot up in bed, startled. A wrenching cry had penetrated her sleep. Disoriented, she craned her neck toward the window. Was she home? Did the scream come from her special window? Was it her father's? She turned on the night lamp by her bed. No, not home. This was Adam's house.

Another roar ripped through the silence.

The hairs on her arms surged upward. She kicked the covers and scrambled to her feet.

A loud thud followed, as if something heavy hit a wall.

She placed her ear to the door. Was Adam having another nightmare?

The slam of a door against its frame vibrated through the panels. It sounded like it came from downstairs, not Adam's bedroom. Was there an intruder in the house? Did he catch him? Trembling, she opened her door and peered out into the hallway.

The door to Adam's room was wide open.

Yasmeen snatched her robe off the chair and inched forward. Pillows lay scattered on the floor. Where did he go? She checked the bathroom. He wasn't there. She contemplated retreating to her room, letting him deal with his nightmare without her interference as she had promised. What if someone broke into the house? Adam was more than capable of overpowering him. What if there were many?

A muffled sound crept up the stairway, a moan or a stifled curse. Could he be hurt? She hurried down the steps, her bare feet transmitting the chill of the floor to her bones. Or was it the other way around? She landed on the last step, looked around in the moonlit living room. Did the sound come from outside?

Framed by the window, a silhouette of a man the size of Adam limped down the porch steps, flailing his arms as if throwing something. He tripped on the last step and fell flat on his back. Sitting up, he bent his knees, placed his hands on the snow-covered ground, and paused for several seconds. Rising, he headed back to the house.

The front door swung open.

She cowered, hiding her body behind the railing.

A gust of cold air blew in with Adam. He stood still, head bowed, a hand on the doorknob keeping it ajar behind him.

She clamped her jaw tight to stop her teeth from making a racket. What was he staring at? Why did he not move?

Lifting his head, Adam closed the door behind him and went into the kitchen.

Leaving her hiding place, she stopped at the kitchen entrance.

Adam stood in front of the stovetop, his back to her. She heard the click of the gas pilot and the glow of cooking fire cast its blue hue around him. He held his hands above the fire. The light wet fabric of his tee-shirt clung to his back, showing trembling muscles underneath.

"I know you're there." His voice crackled like that click of the gas pilot.

"I heard screams."

"We agreed you wouldn't leave your room, no matter what you heard."

"I thought someone broke in."

"You can come in here, there's nothing to be afraid of."

"I was afraid you might be hurt." She took his jacket off the hook by the back door, went to his side, and held it out for him. Her voice dropped to a whisper. "What happened?"

Turning his head away, he took the jacket and slipped it on. "What do you think happened?" He kept his back to her, pulled mugs from a cabinet, and set them on the counter, his movements jerky and almost spastic. "As you can see, I'm fine." He filled the kettle and then set it to boil. "Coffee or tea?"

"Tea, please." She stepped closer, laid a hand on his shoulder. "What were you doing outside?"

Adam placed his elbows on the countertop, pushed his feet back, bending at the waist. He released a shaky sigh. "I was chasing someone." Dipping his head lower, he clasped his hands over the back of his neck. "Out of my head."

She ran her hand across his shoulders. "It is my fault. I reminded you of the war when I asked about your friends."

The kettle whistled. She cut off the gas and carried it to him.

He straightened, taking the kettle from her hand. "It's not your fault. You can't remind me of something I haven't forgotten in the first place. I've had these nightmares ever since I came back from Iraq." He held out one of the full mugs. "If anything, they happen less frequently."

She wrapped cold fingers around the steaming cup, but Adam didn't let go. He leaned in. "Because of you."

"Truly?"

"An observation, that's all." He let go of the cup handle. "Sorry if I scared you again."

"You didn't, I was worried, not scared." Pulling out a chair, she sipped her tea. "Can we call my mother now?"

"Big Scott hasn't emailed me the phone number yet." Adam took the seat across from her. "Give him another hour."

The moon hiding behind tree branches in the back-window cast silver streaks across his face. Yasmeen's fingers itched for her sketchpad to capture the strange image. She flexed her fingers. "Do you own a pistol?"

The cup in Adam's hand stopped short of reaching his lips. "Excuse me?"

"A weapon of any sort?"

"I keep a hunting rifle in the barn." Pushing his chair back, he got to his feet and flipped the light switch. "I keep it unloaded. Safety pin at the locked position. Can't get to it in my sleep, if that's what you're worried about."

She shook her head, realizing he misunderstood her reasons for asking. "No, that is not why I—"

"I will get rid of these nightmares." He ran his hands through his hair, mumbling under his breath. "Now that I have a reason. Just need a little more time."

Yasmeen shot to her feet. "Listen to me. That's not why I asked." She thumbed her chest. "It's for me. I want to use it."

"What?"

"I realized tonight that I am totally dependent on you. If thieves did break in and overpowered you somehow, I have no means to help you."

Like a statue, he stood still, staring at her.

"It would make me feel better knowing I could do something other than hide in a closet."

A muscle around his left eye twitched. "No one's going to break in, rob the house or overpower me." His voice was like a weapon, harsh and cutting.

"I meant no insult. I am trying to be practical. Now that my father has been . . . captured, it is only a matter of time before they get to Fadi." She took a steadying breath. "I don't want to be defenseless when . . . when you are not around."

"I'm not going anywhere." His words were flat, lacking any emotion she could detect.

She touched his arm. "At least, show me where you keep the rifle. Where is the harm in that?"

His eyes roamed over her face, exposing something in their depths that eluded her comprehension. Reluctance? Anger?

"It's not a toy, Yasmeen. It's fucking dangerous."

She dropped her hand to her side. "You seem to

forget where I come from."

He removed his jacket and threw it to a chair. "You'll never need it here."

"I hope I will not."

"When the time's right, I'll teach you how to use the rifle."

"Is it fast like a Kalashnikov? Because I know how to shoot that."

"You what?" His voice went up a couple of decibels, "A Kalashnikov?"

"When I was sixteen, my youngest uncle took me to his brick factory outside the city. He taught me how to fire a Kalashnikov and a hand pistol. He said to keep it to ourselves. I think he did that with all of my cousins."

"Serious?"

"Why would I joke about something like that? I know enough about weapons to wish I never have to use one. But I will if I have to."

The expression in his eyes' depths became clearer.

Disappointment? She turned her face to the window. "I told you I'm not as fragile as you think."

Outside, the world awoke. Birds announced the sun's arrival. Creatures scurried over frozen tree branches. Inside her chest, something tore away and crumbled into many pieces.

Adam approached her from the side. He held her elbows, enticing her to face him.

"Did you have to use one?"

His tone comforted her in a strange way, like that mother's lullaby to her baby drifting through her special window back home, encouraging, and pacifying. Tranquil. The dead were better off, weren't they? They had their peace.

She choked back tears. "How do you think I was able to leave the camp in Turkey without being detected?"

Adam's fingers dug into her skin.

Did he realize he was hurting her? She did not care.

"Fadi bribed a Turkish Red Crescent worker to hide me in his truck. "Two men in black clothes followed the truck to where I was delivered to Fadi in a remote field. He said they were *shabbeeha*, ghostly... shadows. We tried to run, but one of them caught my ankles. I was weak. Not enough food in the camp."

Adam drew her into his arms. "God, I had no idea."

"Fadi hit the man on the head with a big rock. He killed him. The other man attacked Fadi from behind. They wanted him alive to get information."

She buried her face in Adam's chest, wishing she could stop talking.

"It's okay," Adam soothed, caressing her back.

"I used the dead man's gun. Kept firing until it ran out of bullets."

Adam's hands froze. A strange sound emanated from his throat.

"We walked to the nearest farmer's house. He took care of everything for us, burying the bodies, giving us shelter until the paperwork was finalized. He was an angel on earth." Taking a deep breath, she untangled herself from Adam's embrace, reluctant to look at the expression on his face. "I think my uncle prepared me for that day. He knew what was coming."

"I'm so sorry." His voice morphed into someone else's. Foreign. Unrecognizable. Full of repulsion? Disgust? What else could it be after he heard her confess to a murder?

She shuffled out of the kitchen. "You can trust me with your rifle. I know how to use it."

"Yasmeen," Adam called after her.

She paused, a hand on the stairs railing. "We both have things that need to be forgotten. To sleep better."

He limped toward her, his tilted gait more prominent. Was it the weight of her revelation pushing down on him?

"Thank you. For telling me."

Yasmeen dragged her feet up the steps. "Please come get me when it is time to call my mother. I will be wide awake."

CHAPTER 26

A LIE

Blue ocean water broke on the white sand under Yasmeen's feet. She sat by the shore, watching waves advance with the tide and dampen the hem of her dress, her hair blowing in all directions with the warm breeze.

The sun's blazing disc disappeared behind Adam as he approached and towered over her.

"I need them now."

"You can have them." She extended her hand.

Adam took the nails she held and adjusted the bundle of wood boards tucked under his arm.

Digging into the sand with her bare feet, she exposed a hammer buried there. She handed it to Adam, and he dove under the water surface.

He repeatedly came up for air and she tossed him more nails.

"How are you going to get the water out of the box once you are done?"

"I'll burn your dress and let the smoke push it out," he panted, dripping water on her face.

Rising to her feet, she pulled the white cotton dress over her head, balled it and threw it to Adam. The warm breeze turned chilly on her skin.

Adam lit her dress like a torch and took it with him under water.

"Is it working?" Her voice traveled across the waves and echoed to her three times. Is it working? Is it working? Is it working?

Seconds ticked, and he didn't resurface. She dove in after him. Water stung her eyes, but she ignored the pain and strained to see Adam go inside the wood box he made, using her burning dress as a pillow. He smiled, saluted her, and closed the lid. Kicking her feet fast and displacing water with her hands, Yasmeen reached the lid. She held the edges and tried to pry it open with her fingers. She opened her mouth to scream, water rushed into her lungs. Her mind shouted out, "Someone help me," before she felt the tightness in her chest close in.

The lid flew open and floated to the ocean floor with a muffled thud, dispersing clouds of sand her way. She shielded her face with her arm and shouted Adam's name. Her voice came back to her, echoing the name, then gradually fading.

"I'm right here."

"Get out of there, it's not safe." She reached into the box, held his hand and pulled with all her might. His arm ripped off at the shoulder.

"No," she shrieked, held the arm away, the cut where it separated from Adam's shoulder clean, precise, raw. "No. No."

"You're safe." Adam's voice penetrated the water, close to her ear, warm, calm, reassuring.

A strong tide swept her away and deposited her on the dry sand. She opened her eyes. Her hands clung to Adam's arm, her body half raised off the living room couch. She let go, pulled herself to a sitting position and looked around, trying to get oriented.

"What's happening?" Her throat hurt, wounded. Like the day she buried Zainab under the orange tree and tried to say goodbye. Abrasive sounds came out, painful to utter and hear.

"You must've dozed off." Adam lowered his body next to hers on the couch.

"What time is it?"

"Almost five." He switched the light on the corner table to his left.

"Is it morning?"

"Late afternoon. I came home a few minutes ago. Heard you scream." He ran his hand over her hair and rubbed the back of her neck. "Do you remember the dream?"

She shrugged his hand away. "I don't want to

talk about it."

"It's okay, sweetheart." He tried to put his arm around her shoulder.

She hugged her knees to her chest, curling like a ball. Rattled by her cruel dream, she was repulsed by his arm when he tried to hug her. She needed him to go away, so she could regain her composure, breathe easier.

"Aren't you going to take a shower?"

An embarrassed look crossed Adam's face, replacing the worried expression he had. Did she hurt his feelings? The poor man had no idea what he walked into. She couldn't help being rude and abrupt.

He got to his feet. "Sorry. I'm off."

Adam swiped condensed steam off the bathroom mirror. He stared at his distorted reflection and ticked numbers in his head. Taking longer than usual to shower, he tried to give Yasmeen time. It was obvious she didn't want him there, waking up from a nightmare screaming like that. He knew all too well what that was like. Hoping she calmed down enough, he dressed and headed downstairs.

Yasmeen hadn't moved from the couch, curled in the same position he left her in. He hesitated to get closer. "Are you alright?"

She flinched and scurried to her feet. "I meant to clean up before you came down."

Sheets of paper littered the coffee table and the floor area around it. Crayons and coloring pencils scattered out of their boxes.

He approached. "It's okay."

"I let Sara draw here this afternoon until Mr. Abeldeen picked her up." She kneeled and collected the crayons in bundles. Her hands shook, making a bigger mess.

Gathering a stack of papers, he was careful not to get too close.

"I baked a beef and eggplants dish. It will be ready soon. Let me clear this first."

"Got it. Take your time." He went into the kitchen, taking the papers.

"Where are you going with those?"

"Trash."

She hurried after him, snatched the papers out of his hand. "These are Sara's drawings."

The oven timer went off with a loud buzzing sound. She marched past him, slammed the stack of papers on the table, and took out the casserole. "They belong on the refrigerator's door, not in the trash."

Staring at her back, he gritted his teeth. What the hell was going on with her? It couldn't be just the dream. Something else happened.

"They're blank and wrinkled. Sara didn't draw on these."

"It's snow." Yasmeen spread the white pages on the kitchen table and gestured with her hands asking him to come closer. "See?"

Darting his eyes between Yasmeen's angry face and the unmarked pages, he considered possibilities for her odd behavior. Had she connected with her mother on the phone after he left for work? They had tried the number in Big Scott's email many times without luck, and then he had to leave for work. Did they talk? Fight?

"I don't see anything, Yasmeen. Did Sara use some kind of invisible ink?" He decided not to let it go, no matter what kind of conversation she might have had with her mother.

"It needs some imagination, that's all." Yasmeen stomped to the kitchen window facing the back of the house. "Come here. Let me show you."

He strode to the window beside her.

Taking his hand, she kneeled, pulling him down with her. "I asked Sara to draw me a picture of what she saw out this window." She motioned with her head to the glass pane in front of them. "Take a look and tell me what you see."

Piles of snow covered the bottom part of the window. Adam saw only whiteness.

"Now do you understand?" Yasmeen rose to her feet, huffing like a teacher losing patience.

He nodded. Thirty minutes ago, he was insensitive and disgusting, now he was stupid and unimaginative. What else did she have in mind to shoot him down with?

She collected the papers off the table and fixed them on the fridge's door using plastic alphabet magnets. The letters K and L didn't hold the heavy sheets and they tumbled to the floor. She threw down everything in her hands and muttered in Arabic, "*Yila'an hal dinya.*"

Using the windowsill for support, he rose. He didn't know what the words meant, but the tone of her voice and the redness in her face told him they must be curse words. This was the first time he saw her lose control like that.

"What happened today?" He made sure his tone was serious enough to demand her attention. "What's wrong?"

"Everything," Yasmeen yelled and covered her face with her hands. "Everything is wrong, and I don't know what to do."

A dreadful feeling twisted his insides. "There's

nothing inside the fridge except food, Yasmeen. You need to get over this."

"It is not the fridge," she mumbled behind her hands.

He stepped closer, held her wrists, and peeled her palms away from her face. "Did you talk to your mother? Is that it?" He kept her hands in his.

She nodded, leaned back against the fridge, and fixed her eyes on a spot above his shoulder. Tears ran down her cheeks.

"Mother thinks I live with a kind family who has a daughter my age. She doesn't know about you. Last time she heard from Fadi, he simply told her I was taken care of. He didn't tell her how I left Turkey to get here." Yasmeen closed her eyes. "She thinks a generous family of Syrian origin sponsored me to go to school."

He rubbed her wedding ring under his thumb. "What did she say when you told her the truth?"

Yasmeen's lower lip trembled. She bit it and turned her head to the side.

Realization churned in his stomach like grinding stones. "You never told her."

"I couldn't." She pulled her hands out of his, dragged her feet and slumped onto the nearest chair. "I didn't know where to start. She expects me to join her soon."

He stood rooted in his spot, empty hands retreated into the back pockets of his pants, eyes fixed on the fridge's yellow ugliness. "Call her tomorrow and explain the situation."

"She has a suitor lined up for me." Yasmeen's voice dropped to a whisper. "A nice Syrian doctor from a good family."

Adam turned to look at her, his mind frozen, refusing to process what he heard.

"Mother sounded . . . hopeful. How can I tell her I already have a husband?" Yasmeen's voice shook. "I can't, Adam. It will destroy her." She pressed both hands on her abdomen. "I am the reason she has not slipped into despair after Father's arrest and Fadi's absence. She is counting on my return."

"And planning your wedding." He tasted the bitterness that came out with his words.

"Please try to understand," Yasmeen pleaded. "I can't . . . hurt my mother. I have to go to her."

He limped to the back door and ripped it open, feeling like he'd aged several years. "You forgot one thing. You have to get a divorce first."

***

Pacing the floor, Yasmeen checked her watch for what seemed the hundredth time. The green florescent glow of the microwave clock confirmed the late hour, fifteen minutes past midnight. She was going out of her mind with worry.

Where could he be?

Since Adam stormed out earlier in the evening, she spent time reasoning her way to a decision. She made a list in her head for the many reasons she should leave as planned: This masquerade of a marriage which Adam deserved none of, the absence of suspected danger to her life in Jordan, the financial and emotional support she would give her mother in these terrible times, and most importantly, a return to familiarity.

She yearned to live in her own skin again, to express herself in a language where she wouldn't fear misunderstandings. She missed the little details in everyday living, searching for missing spices and hoping for other ingredients in the food she ate. Or listening to the sounds of nature waiting for prayer calls from mosque minarets to interrupt the monotony and establish a rhythm for her day. Or walking down the street to the neighborhood bookstore to buy the latest poetry book and discuss it with her friends. She longed for the smells and sounds of busy markets, to be drawn into a shop by a song played through loud speakers, or the promise of a great deal because she went to school with the owner's daughter.

She thought of the small bursts of beauty shining through a world dominated by chaos. Small stitches that wove the fabric of her life became undone in this place. Just as she started knotting new ones with Adam, an opportunity to wrap herself in a familiar cloth had presented itself. How could she turn it down?

Outside, flakes of snow danced their way to the ground. A sense of belonging plagued her. Where did she fit on this new land?

And what about that man her mother had in line for her, another stranger for a husband. Would he love her? Would he be as considerate as Adam? As accepting of her, knowing she had lived under the roof of another man, an American? It would be easy to omit that fact, since nothing physical happened between them. But what about that kiss Adam gave her? Was that the right way to describe it? Something granted, like a gift? It felt that way. Did it count? How could it not, when every moment since that night she relived it in her head? What kind of person would she be if she started a new life with a lie?

Dangling from a hook by the back door, Adam's car keys caught her eye. Had he walked to the Abeldeens' house? She disregarded that possibility.

Adam would not intrude on that family this late at night.

Darting to the other window, she checked the barn lights. All of them were off. She flipped the switch for the floodlight on top the barn. Nothing moved other than the tabby fur ball sauntering across the yard. If only she learned how to drive. She could take the car to look for him instead of sitting here going crazy.

Her stomach jumped and she pressed a hand to it. She turned to the phone. Should she try his cell phone? She tapped her fingers on the handset. What would she say if he answered the call? *Come home, you can have your life back?*

Biting the inside of her cheek, she dialed his cell number. The familiar ringtone beckoned her from the living room. Dejected, she followed the sound to the armed chair by the fireplace where Adam's cell phone sang under the cushions, mocking her.

***

Earnest trotted with caution in falling snow. The stubborn horse refused to cross the small bridge leading to the cemetery. The animal shook his head as if expressing his disapproval at the danger of being outdoors in this weather. Adam should heed his warning and turn back to the house. He nudged Earnest forward with the tips of his boots and relaxed the reins in his hands, encouraging him with words he responded to.

The horse galloped forward, his breath dispersing clouds of tiny water droplets around his head. They reached the iron gates of the square enclosure. Adam turned on his flashlight and pointed it through the gates. An ancient tree spread its bare branches in the center of the cemetery, dark and ominous, guarding the souls under her roots.

Adam dismounted and tied the rains to one of the gate's poles. He pushed the gate open and tucked the flashlight under one arm to warm his hands in his jacket pockets.

Snow buried headstones, covering almost everything in sight. Concrete angels poked their heads above the white mounds in the distance. He cut through the middle of the square to his destination and placed the flashlight by his feet at the right angle. Kneeling, he pushed aside snow with his bare hands, and realized the stupidity of his actions. He lost feeling in his fingers, yet barely uncovered the top of the granite headstone. He got to his feet, the soaked fabric of his pants sticking to his skin. He cupped his palms in front of his mouth and blew some warmth onto them, then tucked them under his armpits to keep from shivering.

"I know what you're going say, Mom," he addressed the cleared spot of the headstone. "Always keep your promises. Look where it got me."

Shifting his eyes to a point to his right, he strained to see through the cast shadows of the branches above. "Grandpa was right. Doing the right thing doesn't always take you to the right place." He shook his legs to generate some heat. "Maybe it's time to take a wrong turn, see where it would lead."

Some creature of the night stirred on a high branch, an owl or a bat. "Don't worry, Mom. If Yasmeen wants to fly, I won't clip her wings like Fred did to you."

CHAPTER 27

A TURN

The silhouette of man and horse appeared in the distance. Yasmeen breathed a sigh of relief when she saw them head toward the barn. With the lights on inside the house and out, she had no doubt Adam saw her standing by the kitchen window. Pretending otherwise would be stupid. She planted her feet in front of the back door and waited for him to walk in, fully prepared to give the speech in her head.

Long agonizing minutes later, Adam faced Yasmeen under the kitchen lights. His nose, chin, and ears were bright red, his hair wet, and the legs of his pants stiff with mud.

She forgot the beginning of her speech. "I will warm up dinner while you change."

"Don't bother." He removed his boots. "Not hungry."

She turned to the sink and filled the water kettle. "How about hot tea?"

"No. I need a shower." He headed to the stairway.

Yasmeen hurried after him. "Can we talk when you are done?"

Placing his foot on the first step, he kept his head down. "There's no need. I know what you want. I'll contact Sam in the morning and have him send the divorce papers." He climbed two steps at once. "Don't know if he did anything with the residency application yet, but we'll deal with it in due time. I'll work out your travel details with Big Scott. Probably take a few weeks." Reaching the top of the stairs, Adam looked down at her. "Can you wait that long?"

Her face flamed as if he slapped her. That was it, then? He wasn't going to try to talk her out of it, or ask her to reconsider? He didn't prepare his own list to convince her to stay? She didn't get to deliver her speech, either. She felt cheated, and embarrassed, and many other things she would not confess.

"Yasmeen?"

She flinched. "That will be fine."

Everything was in order. Yasmeen informed Mrs. Abeldeen not to send Sara for her art class, the house chores were taken care of, including dinner plans, and Amy was on her way to pick up Yasmeen to spend the day in town. She needed the distraction, a break from a mental conversation that almost always ended with the same question, *what do I do now?*

On the fridge, a note from Adam said he needed to visit the vet in town to make arrangements for vaccinations for the herd. Not knowing what to say, she'd stayed in bed on purpose until she heard him leave the house. She climbed into Amy's car, determined to have a good time, and pushed the issue of the divorce to the back of her mind.

"What's the plan?" Amy ran a red stick over her lips, checking her precision in the visor mirror.

"I'm up for anything." Yasmeen forced a smile and tried to interject a measure of carelessness in her tone. "At some point, I would like to stop at Blooms Boutique to return a few items."

"What, they don't fit? You gained some weight?"

She folded her arms on her chest. "A little. They are new and I will never wear them." She liked that explanation, decided to stick with it in case Amy prodded further about her desire to reduce her wardrobe.

"Let's hope Maryanne will be at the store today." Amy drove off. "She hired Pamela Phelps to help her manage the business. Don't want to deal with that woman."

"Why?"

"Let's just say we weren't best friends in high school. She had perfect teeth, flawless skin, blond curls. Made every girl around her feel like the ugly duckling."

Yasmeen had no idea what duckling meant, but she guessed at Amy's point. "Does that mean the girls were jealous?"

"More like invisible. Every guy in school had eyes for Miss Perfect Pamela. She loved the attention, encouraged it, flirted all the time. I'm telling you, she's one to watch out for."

After a couple of stops in town, they entered Mrs. Dawson's salon.

"I'm going for a new look." Yasmeen pulled out her hair tie. "Let us cut it off, Mrs. Dawson. Like that one on the wall." She pointed at a poster of a model with short spiky hair.

"Let's not go overboard here." Amy flipped through a magazine and showed her a couple of pictures of less severe, feminine hairstyles. They agreed on one, and Mrs. Dawson went to work.

Satisfied with her new look, Yasmeen left the salon, feeling lighter and younger.

"You should've had your hair done this way long time ago." Amy pushed open the door to Blooms Boutique. "It brings out your eyes."

"I need to get used to it."

The doorbell announced their entry but didn't beckon anyone to greet them. They heard muffled voices at the back of the shop and headed in that direction. Amy stopped at one of the racks to examine a blouse, while Yasmeen continued on. The voices became clearer, a man cursed many times, and a woman laughed. A brazen, unabashed laugh.

In a corner by the fitting room, a woman with long blond curls nestled in the lap of a man, his knees slightly bent, face hidden by the fitting room curtain.

Yasmeen berated herself for the intrusion. Trying to retreat, her foot bumped something solid. A box flipped over and hit the floor with a loud thump.

Still laughing, the slender woman turned and, without shame, fixed the top of her dress to cover a good portion of her bosom.

The man pulled away from the corner and turned around. Yasmeen came face-to-face with Adam. A deep blush crept up his neck. Yasmeen's lungs inflated with a sharp intake of air, her knees locked, gluing her feet to the floor.

Amy came up behind her and stopped short. Her mouth fell open. "Pamela."

"Hey there, Anne?" Pamela cracked a smile. "I didn't hear you come in. I'll be with you in a second."

"It's Amy. This is Jasmine." Amy narrowed her eyes and pointed at Adam. "His wif—"

"How can I help you?" Pamela cut her off, fluffed her hair, and sashayed toward the front of the shop.

Amy punched him in the arm. "What the hell, Adam?"

He barely moved.

Speechless, Yasmeen turned, maneuvered her way to the front, and stumbled out the door. Tears collected in her eyes and distorted everything in her sight. She scrubbed her eyes with her scarf and hurried to the diner across the street.

Slipping into a booth by the window, she saw Amy dash out of the shop and look up and down the street. An overwhelming sensation of disappointment pushed down on Yasmeen, making her feel small and unimportant. It was not Adam who came after her. Shoulders hunched, she got up, opened the diner door and signaled Amy to join her.

"I swear, we're back in high school again," Amy huffed as soon as she sat across from Yasmeen. "You okay, honey?" She touched Yasmeen's arm.

Yasmeen looked toward the shop again. "He is still in there." Her throat worked hard to swallow a lump.

"How can you be so calm? If Jonathan did that to me, I'd pull Miss Perfect Pamela's hair out one curl at a time, and then I'd bite him as hard as I can. On his face so everyone knows what he did."

Tears flowed from Yasmeen's eyes. Dear God, was that all she would do?

"Don't know what got into him," Amy brought her tone down. "I've known Adam for a long time. He's not the sort of guy who'd behave this way. And he just stood there, didn't say a word."

"He's making a point." Yasmeen used a paper napkin to wipe her tears.

"What, that he's a jerk?"

"He's fed up with me." Yasmeen twisted the napkin in her hands. "He has done his duty toward my brother, and now he's ready to go back to his own life."

"Pamela was never part of his life, for Heaven's sake. Trust me, I know. If they were ever involved, Miss Perfect Pamela would've made sure everyone in town knew about it." Amy leaned across the table and prompted Yasmeen to look at her. "Adam didn't behave this way when he was single, now that he's married to you, he does this? Turns into a moron?" She sat back and shook her head. "It doesn't add up."

"I pushed him to it. I told him last night I needed to go to my mother in Jordan."

Amy arched her eyebrows. "Why did you tell him that?"

"Because my mother expects me."

"I don't understand. Why?"

"It's complicated. There's a lot you don't know about my . . . situation." She took a deep breath and cleared her throat. "It's over. I can't impose on him any longer. I have to go."

Amy pointed her index finger in her face. "Do you *want* to go?"

The question felt like a smack to the back of her head. The list of reasons she had in her mind appeared in front of her eyes. The napkin in her hands disintegrated to tiny pieces.

"It doesn't matter what I want. Where I come from, you do what is expected. Family comes before everything."

Amy snatched the remaining pieces of the destroyed napkin from Yasmeen's hands. "Honey, until this moment, Adam has been your family too."

"Obviously, he doesn't see it that way." Spit flew from Yasmeen's mouth with her words. Placing her elbows on the table, she covered her face with her palms and breathed deep to squash the boiling anger inside her.

"Do you think there are others?"

"I don't think—"

Adam's voice seared through her like lightning. "There's no one."

CHAPTER 28

A LAKE

Placing both hands flat on the table, Adam bent closer to Yasmeen's hidden face. "Let's go home."

Amy glared at him. "I'll drop her off later."

"Stay out of this, Amy."

"I don't think you're in a position to demand anything right now."

He straightened. "This is between me and *my wife*."

Amy huffed. "Now you remember?"

Yasmeen lowered her hands and turned to the window. "Amy, please. This's not the place."

Adam couldn't see her face.

She grabbed her purse and scooted out of the booth. "I am going home. I will call you tomorrow, okay?"

Amy stepped around him and hugged Yasmeen. "Give him hell."

Holding the door open, he waited for Yasmeen to walk out, and noticed she avoided looking at him. The same thing happened when he opened the car door for her. He heaved a long breath, braced himself, and got behind the wheel. A couple of minutes into the ride, he glanced at her, sitting stiff, her shoulders squared, and her head held high.

"You got a haircut."

She nodded, staring straight ahead.

"It's nice." He waited for a response, but Yasmeen didn't utter a sound. "Makes you look younger." He placed check marks next to bullet points in his head: looks, age. What else could he bring up to soften a woman's edges?

"And thinner," he added.

Frowning, Yasmeen turned her head and leveled icy eyes on him. Realizing she saw right through his ridiculous attempt to gain favor, he cleared his throat.

"You alright?"

"Why wouldn't I be?" Her words sounded forceful, rather than nonchalant.

"We're going to play games now?"

"Speak plainly, please. So, I can understand you. I'm not in the mood to guess at what you mean."

"Fine." He steered the car to the shoulder and slammed on the brakes. "You're upset by what you saw."

Yasmeen raised her voice. "You couldn't wait

until I was gone?"

"Don't jump to conclusions," he stressed each word. "Let me explain—"

She cut him off. "No need to explain the obvious."

"I walked into the store, saw Pamela—"

"I know what I saw," she interjected, almost yelling.

"Saw her reach for a box on top of a shelf. I tried to—"

"You had to hurt me like that?" Yasmeen placed her hand on her chest, continuing with her tirade as if he wasn't speaking.

He paused. Stretching his arm to the back of her seat, he leaned closer. "Why are you hurt?"

Yasmeen scooted back until her head pressed at the window. "Any woman would be insulted by what you did."

"Why should *you* care?"

"I'm still your wife, and unless those papers that say otherwise are finalized, I expect you to honor that fact. Not act like a . . . a . . . a rafe."

"You mean like a *rake*." He drew back. Shit, why'd that have to slip out?

Yasmeen threw her hands in the air. "Whatever," she shouted. "You know what I mean. Doing what bad men do."

He counted to ten in his head, attempting to remain calm. "I tried to help Pamela reach a box, and she cornered me."

"The woman was on top of you." She spread her hands over her chest. "All exposed."

"She came on to me." He dragged his eyes away from Yasmeen's angry face. "I was trapped."

"And you couldn't shove Miss Perfect Pamela away, could you?"

He shook his head. "I try hard not to lay my hands on a woman that way."

"That's not what I meant," Yasmeen's voice faltered.

"You . . . you could have pushed her away."

"Didn't touch her," he exploded, his control shot to hell.

"I don't believe you."

"Believe what you like. Don't see why it matters."

She fidgeted, pulling on the seatbelt away from her chest. "I expect a principled man like you would manage the situation better. If that's truly what happened."

A car passed by and sprayed Adam's window with dirty snow. "Disappointment is a bitch, isn't it?"

Confusion swept over her face.

"Hasn't anyone ever told you not to expect much of people? Told you from the beginning, I'm not good company. Don't blame me if you refused to believe me."

She twisted the fringes of her scarf between her fingers. "You were the right company for me."

Adam breathed in deep. There's that soothing balm again, cooling another burn.

"Until today." Her voice broke, as if the words forced their way out against her will.

He exhaled her name.

"Do you have a relationship with that woman?"

"I've known Pamela for years. Never been in a relationship. Didn't even know she worked there."

"You went to see Maryanne, didn't you?"

"Only to talk."

"You expect me to believe you?"

"I expect you to *understand*. I needed to be where I felt . . . wanted."

"How would you feel if the situation was reversed?

Would you be understanding toward me?"

"Last night, you told me you wouldn't tell your mother about us. That you wanted to leave and marry another man. How do you think that made me feel?"

"I didn't say I want to leave." She unfastened

her seatbelt and opened the car door. "I said I *have* to leave." Her boots skidded on the snow, struggling to move away from the car.

It took him a few seconds to absorb her words. She didn't want to leave? He turned off the car and stumbled out. Freezing wind lashed at him. The sound of her boots crunching snow loud and prominent in the absence of other noises. Not a tree for the wind to ruffle. Not even birds flew above. Nothing moved in the arid space other than this delicate, dark-haired woman, who fought so hard to keep from being vulnerable. As hard as he did. Maybe even harder. He spent his entire life locked in that battle, and where did it land him? The woman who accepted his deficiencies, who stitched closed his raw wounds, was walking away from him.

"Hold on." He tried to catch up with her. "Where're you going?"

"Home," she shouted over her shoulder, and continued to move into the open. "Oh, wait. I can't go home, can I? I don't *have* a home."

"Don't go any further."

"Leave me alone." She picked up her pace.

Closing the distance, he grabbed her arm. "Stop it." He swung her around. "This's a lake. Ice is thin."

Planting her hands on his chest, she locked her elbows. "Don't touch me."

"Listen to me." He shook her. "It's dangerous to stand here."

"Let go." She twisted her body sideways, pulling away.

"Damn it woman, what do you want from me?"

Yasmeen fell back, legs flailing in the air. Cracking sounds echoed, deep and distant.

He thrust out his hands, reaching for her. She swatted them aside, rolled to her knees and brought herself to her feet. Bending forward, she brushed the front of her jeans.

"You alright?" His voice laced with panic.

Her head jerked upward. "No, I'm not alright. I'm wet and cold and humiliated."

The cracking sounds echoed louder this time. A dark spot in the frozen surface behind Yasmeen grew wider and spread like a spider web toward her feet.

He snatched her hand. "Hurry!"

Cursing under his breath, Adam ran a hand through his hair, and counted backwards to bring down his racing pulse. If he had been a moment too late, he would not have been able to pull Yasmeen to solid ground when her legs plunged into the water.

Out of breath and shivering, Yasmeen craned her neck, looking back at the cracking ice as the car sped away. "That was c-close." Her teeth chattered. "I d-don't know how to s-swim."

Panic had trapped air in his lungs. He cracked his window and gulped fresh air.

"Can you p-please close t-that? I am c-cold."

"Give me a Goddamn minute, will you? We'll be home soon. Take off your pants."

"I will do no s-such thing."

"You'll warm up faster." He closed the window and cranked up the heat. "Brought the bags you left in Maryanne's shop. In the back seat. Change into something dry."

She didn't move.

Leaning closer to the wheel, sharp pain stabbed his leg. He winced, peeled off his jacket and handed it to her.

"Cover yourself with this, if that's what's stopping you." Shit, he intended to be encouraging. But damn it, his tone was abrasive. He tried again. "Please, you don't want to get sick."

Reaching toward the back, Yasmeen dug in a bag and pulled out a pair of pants. She removed her wet boots and socks, then spread his jacket on her lap. The process of wiggling out of her wet jeans in that awkward setting added to his irritation. He kept his eyes on the road ahead, not wanting to watch. But he couldn't stop glancing her way across the car seat. What was so complicated? Her trembling hands kept tugging on the sides of his jacket to keep most of her legs covered until she slipped the dry pants on.

"Any socks in those bags?" He clenched his jaw many times.

"No."

"Wrap my jacket around your feet."

"My scarf is dry. I will use it." She handed him back his jacket.

He laid it across his lap. Simple movement became painful, his left leg muscles contracted and shot a burning sensation to his foot. Cold, anger, tension, even fear disturbed his mind and body. Unable to concentrate and drive safely, he slowed down, parked the car on the shoulder again.

"Why are we stopping?"

Tilting his seat, he stretched his leg as far as he could and rested his head. "Just need a minute."

"Is it your leg?"

"Yup." How could he explain to her that the pain ran deeper than his muscles? Way near to his heart? Coming close to losing her in the lake brought back painful memories. He didn't want to lose her. Period.

"You warming up?"

She reached for the heat controls and dialed down the fan. "Do you mind? I'm hot."

"Don't mind that at all." He studied her profile, convinced her innocent mind missed his meaning. She had a point. He could have handled the situation with Pamela better. The woman started flirting with him the instant he walked into the shop. He should have anticipated what was coming. What a fool, letting her push him around like an adolescent boy. Pamela was determined. Saw it in her eyes, and he liked the attention. Yasmeen wanted to leave him, and he was no angel. Nothing but a Goddamn fool. A bad seed.

"I'm sorry." He heard his father's voice in his head, saying the same useless words to his mother. Bile lurched up from his stomach and he swallowed it down.

"I fell. It wasn't your fault. You tried to warn me."

"About Pamela. Could've found a way to avoid what happened. Didn't mean for us to get to this point." Bringing his seat upright again, he held her hand. "Be honest with me. I understand why you're angry. There's stuff—"

"You were wrong, Adam." Her voice was low,

it seemed dangerously low, like something else was on her mind. "It wasn't disappointment that made me angry. It was . . . Mr. Abeldeen."

"What?"

Tapping on Adam's window, Ben shouted, "You alright in there?"

Adam rolled down his window. "Hey, man."

"Somethin' wrong with the car?"

"My leg's acting up. Good thing you came by. Can you give us a ride home?"

"Sure. Junior and me will come back for your car."

"You could've warned me." Adam turned off the car engine.

"His face appeared out of nowhere." Yasmeen sounded inpatient.

"You were about to say something before Ben showed up? What was it that—"

She placed her hand on the door handle. "I want to go, please."

He swallowed the rest of his words. So she wanted to leave, after all. Frustrated, he slammed the wheel with his fist. "Your boots are still wet. Don't get out, I'll come around and carry you to Ben's truck." By the time he limped over to her side, Yasmeen had slipped her bare feet into her boots.

"I will walk over."

Yasmeen scooted on the long leather seat to the middle. The scratched muddy truck had a warm and welcoming feeling. Adam squeezed his body in after her, put one arm around her shoulder, gluing her to his side.

The men talked weather and farm business. She listened to none of it, her mind analyzing new realities. Admitting the reason behind her outrage surprised her. She was jealous, no question about it. She had to acknowledge a more basic emotion driving that jealousy. The feeling settled in her core, a wondrous entity, planting hope and weeding out resistance. It spread warmth and shifted everything into focus.

Deep down inside, she believed his account of what happened at Maryanne's shop. Adam proved himself to be a principled man so far, a desired man. She needed to face the facts. The idea of him holding another woman painted agonizing details in her mind. It didn't matter to her if it was Miss Perfect Pamela or Mrs. Maryanne Merick. It could have been a dazzling genie, for all she cared. She should be the one who ignited his passion.

Pressed into Adam's side, something novel and strange occurred. His voice close to her ear seemed to tease while he talked. The fabrics between their skins appeared to have vanished. The weight of his arm draped over her shoulder jarred her, as if it connected with her bones. What was happening to her?

She studied every detail of his profile while he conversed with Mr. Abeldeen. A powerful craving for his full attention engulfed her. An intense desire to discover unknown pleasures through his touch sharpened her senses. Tilting her head to rest it on his shoulder, she felt his pulse in her veins. Who was this hypersensitive creature? Was it really her?

The many reasons to leave she had listed in her mind dispersed like coffee residue in a fortune-teller's upturned coffee cup, leaving incomprehensible squiggles and lines. A hunger to experience something entirely fresh, without remnants of loud memories or scary dreams, burned all doubts away. Her mother was a woman. She would understand. She would want this for her.

Adam gazed at her and grinned. It struck at her heart and made her wonder if he sensed a change in her, or if he suddenly developed superpowers that read her mind. An urge overwhelmed her, causing her to become possessive and greedy. Why did it have to be one or the other? Why couldn't she have both? She considered possibilities of what to do about her mother and Adam, how to bring the two of them to the same place. Did Adam still want her, and how could she change his mind if he didn't? All she needed was a bit of courage at the right moment.

Adam coughed into his closed fist. She tried to pay attention, to catch up.

"Should I place the order?" Mr. Abeldeen was asking.

"Yeah." Adam's tone was strange, as if he was fighting to breath. Giving her a quick tug with his arm, he raised his eyebrows.

At a loss, Yasmeen thought he probably sought some comment from her, and tried to concentrate on what Mr. Abeldeen talked about, something that had to do with syringes, two hundred of them. What were syringes, anyway? Did they mean injections?

Adam's leg twitched next to hers, she looked down. To her utter embarrassment, she found she had been caressing his thigh. His inner thigh. Feeling flames about to erupt from her cheeks, she snatched her wandering hand, hid it between her knees, and fixed her eyes on the road ahead for the rest of the way.

Mr. Abeldeen turned the truck into the driveway leading to the house. A white van came into view, parked in the square. "Looks like you have company."

"Don't know anyone who owns a van like that." Adam jumped out of the truck.

The front door of the house swung open. Fred Shipman stepped out, cupped his hand in front of his mouth and lit a cigarette.

CHAPTER 29

A NIGHT

Adam planted his feet by the truck, fists tight, and stared at Fred on the porch. A short, round woman was poised behind the screen door, with two small heads on either side of her skirt.

Yasmeen stumbled out of the truck and positioned herself in front of him. "Look at me," she whispered.

It took him a couple of seconds to tear his eyes away and look down at her.

"There are children in the house." She placed both hands on his chest. "They are guests in our home. Please be civil."

Adam frowned. Did she say *our* home? He relaxed his fists. "Give me a little more credit, okay?"

Ben came to his side. "Shall I call the Sherriff?"

"I can handle this." Adam handed him his car keys.

He took hold of Yasmeen's hand, and went up the steps leading to the porch.

"What the hell are you doing here?"

"I knew you weren't gonna invite me, so I acted. Brought the family to meet you." Fred blew smoke circles. The children giggled behind the mesh screen.

"Your sisters, Emma and Julie." Fred dropped his cigarette to the porch floor and stepped on the butt. "My wife Lisa, your stepmom, I guess."

Adam opened the screen door. Lisa and the girls retreated as he entered, pulling Yasmeen with him. Something about the way Lisa stood, half hidden by the girls, made him feel uneasy about the woman. Lisa ran nervous blue eyes over him. His unwelcoming frown most likely intimidated her.

Fred's voice came from behind. "You never told me your name."

"My name is Yasmeen." Her hand still in Adam's, she bent to one knee, addressing the girls. "I have cookies in the kitchen. Would you like some?"

The children bobbed their heads and looked up at their mother for permission. Lisa nodded, her mouth breaking into a wide smile.

Adam scowled. How could a smile make any woman look more unappealing?

Before Yasmeen took the girls into the kitchen, she turned to the woman, "Lisa, would you like to join us?"

"Go on." Fred ordered with a flick of his hand. Lisa complied.

Clenching his mouth shut, Adam went to poke at the logs in the fireplace.

Fred made a slow circle around the living room and stopped in front of the fireplace to face him. "Like what you did to the house. Looks . . . new. Surprised you didn't change the lock, though."

Seeing his father inside the house again after all those years wrought havoc on his nerves, and he wasn't in the right frame of mind. Yasmeen's contradicting actions and comments chipped at his ability to concentrate.

"Notice I didn't smoke inside? Remembered how you hated that."

"What do you want?" Adam crossed his arms, not bothering to acknowledge Fred's feeble attempt to appease him.

Fred took a step closer. "Hear me out, okay?" He glanced toward the kitchen. "I appreciate you not makin' a scene in front of my girls."

He gave a curt nod.

"I didn't like the way we left things in Chicago. Believe it or not, I wanna smooth things over with you."

"Why?"

Fred dropped his head, checking his boots. "Lisa and the girls may need you after I'm gone."

"You planning on leaving them? You sick or something?" He made sure his voice lacked compassion.

"Nothin' like that." Fred cleared his throat. "You're the only family they got."

Inhaling, Adam summoned some control, and waited for Fred to lift his head. "You never showed that kind of consideration for my mother. She didn't have family here either."

"I'm tryin' to do better this time around. Look, I know I was hard on you and . . . Betty, but the Lord's forgiven me. Surely you can too, if you try?"

"Why should I?" He unfolded his arms and pointed a finger at Fred. "So, you can sleep better at night?"

Sounds of laughter drifted from the kitchen. Yasmeen's singing voice merged with the uninhibited giggles of the little girls. Lisa's voice was absent.

"You're out of luck, old man. I'm not that charitable."

"You're a family man now. I'd like to see you do better than—"

With one quick move, he grasped Fred's shoulders. "You have until the end of the day, and then you'll take your family back to Chicago. My wife is having too much fun with those girls for me to ruin it for her now."

"Those girls are your sisters." Fred's defiance showed on his face and in his tone.

"Because you say so? I didn't ask for sisters." With his thumbs, he applied the right amount of pressure on Fred's vulnerable spots by his collarbone.

Fred withered.

Living on the farm, Adam never thought he might use his military training on anyone, least of all his father. "If I ever find out you touched as much as a hair on either one of them in any threatening way, I'll make sure you regret showing your face here today." He dropped his hands just before the point he knew would render Fred unconscious.

Fred staggered back and used the wall for support. "I was hoping you'd say that."

"What the fuck does that mean?"

"I need to be accountable to someone who knows what I can do." He rubbed the sore spots. "To stop me, if I screw up."

Adam leaned closer, bringing his nose within inches of Fred's. "Don't you dare make this my responsibility, you manipulative piece of shit. You have no idea what *I'm* capable of, so don't try me. If I have to do it again, I'll stop you for good. Do we understand each other?" He backed away just as the women and children entered the room.

"I need to change my clothes." Yasmeen connected eyes with his. Turning away, he pretended to examine the fire.

"I will be back in five minutes." She ran up the stairs.

Fred sat on the couch, opened his arms inviting his daughters. The girls ran to him.

"What kinda cookies did you have?" He hugged them closer.

"Chocolate chip." The youngest ran the back of her hand over her mouth, wiping none of the milk mustache she had.

"Yummy?" Fred poked her stomach.

"Soft and mushy, just like mommy makes them," the older one answered.

Adam felt out of place, the scene unfolding in front of him was foreign. He turned his attention to Lisa. The smile on her face perplexed him. A woman smiling at Fred? How was that possible?

"How old are you, Emma?" Adam tried to figure out which girl was which.

"Five," the girl on Fred's right said. She had her mother's eyes and brown hair.

"And you?" He smiled at Julie. She lifted three chubby fingers. Long bangs covered most of her eyes. Her smile matched her father's.

Emma pointed a finger at him. "You walk funny."

"Yup." Adam tapped his leg, unsure if the child picked up on his growing discomfort. Didn't children have the ability to see through people? Something about their untainted senses?

"Accident?" Fred kept his eyes on his daughters, didn't bother to look at him.

His lips closed tight. Fred didn't know Adam served in the army, almost died in Iraq. Would he have cared? He waited for Fred to ask more questions, find out about his so-called accident. Nothing.

Lisa approached the trio and balanced her plump body on the couch's arm. She leaned over and kissed her husband.

A strange feeling descended on Adam and prevented him from holding his stance. The image of his father lovingly holding his children didn't fit in this living room. Maybe it's because they're girls. No need for Fred to act tough in order to make men out of them. Feeling like an intruder, he excused himself and took the steps upstairs two-at-a-time, ignoring the pain in his leg. He found Yasmeen outside her room, dressed in a fresh pair of jeans and a blue shirt.

"Did I take too long? I was just about to—"

He reached for her and folded his body into hers. The act lacked tenderness. A surprised 'oomph' escaped her throat. She lifted her hands to his back and let him hold her longer than he expected.

"No matter how you look at it, that's your family downstairs."

"Not really," Adam choked.

"Your sisters, Adam. Invite Fred and Lisa to stay until tomorrow. It is cruel to have them drive those children through the night."

He felt like a child being pacified in her arms. Taking a deep breath, he pulled back. "Is that what you want?"

She arched her eyebrows. "Please?"

"Then you invite them. This is your home too."

"You mean it?"

Words stuck in his throat. He nodded.

"You will not mind?"

"Not if it makes you happy."

She lifted up on her toes and kissed his cheek. "Thank you, you will not regret it."

Watching her hop downstairs, he wondered if she realized he would put up with the devil himself if she asked him.

***

The happy chaos that accompanied children spread throughout the house, putting Adam on edge. The girls chased each other around furniture pieces and squealed when they tripped and fell. The women occupied the kitchen, busy preparing dinner, chatting non-stop. Lisa's high-pitched voice aggravated him the most. Fred disappeared into the basement after Adam had asked him to take a look at some of his old stuff. He needed to keep Fred out of his sight. Mr. Abeldeen dropped off the car and offered to cover his afternoon shift. Adam remained indoors with a watchful eye on Emma and Julie.

The phone rang, and he was thankful for the interruption. Barely hearing Sam's voice over the loud shrieks of the girls, he took his jacket and stepped outside.

"Did you get the papers I sent you?"

"Yes. I'm waiting on one last document before I file everything with INS. But something strange happened you should know about."

"What?"

"I sent a routine request to the Syrian Embassy for a no-criminal history document on Miss Jabir. Should have received it by now. Instead, I got this call from a man at the embassy asking to have her contact them directly. It's never happened in any of the immigration cases I handled before. I sent a letter of representation as usual with my request, so there shouldn't have been a problem. Embassies usually send the document either clearing the person or informing of a record."

"What did you tell him?"

"I asked him if she had a criminal record. He said he would only talk to Miss Jabir. I told him that I'm her attorney, and I'll handle all communications on her behalf. He hung up."

Apprehension gripped Adam's stomach. "What's the guy's name?"

"Haytham Al Afandy."

"Spell it." He wrote the name in the condensation on the back windowpane. "Did you have our address on anything you sent them?"

"No. Everything goes through my office."

"Did my name appear anywhere on that request letter, or the fact that she's married to me?"

"There's no need. It's a simple request form. It doesn't mention on what grounds we're applying to the INS, and it shouldn't concern them one bit. To tell you the truth, I'm surprised the Syrian embassy is still operating with all that's going on over there."

"Are you sure this Al Afandy guy was from the

embassy?" He wiped the name with his sleeve.

"I checked. Called back and asked for his name, they put me through to his voicemail. He works there, for sure. At what level, I have no idea."

Sweat broke out on Adam's forehead. He ran a hand through his hair. "Listen, can you file the immigration papers without that document?"

"I might be able to get around it, given some leeway INS is granting Syrian citizens because of the current situation. It would have been easier had we requested a refugee status. But that's not the case. A spousal visa adjustment is different. It would help if you send me a couple of letters testifying to her good character from people who know her here. But it's going to cost us time."

"And time's money. I understand. Got you covered. I'll send those letters to you in a couple of days. Just do it, please."

Adam looked through the window into the kitchen. Yasmeen carried a steaming pot from the stovetop to the sink and saw him. She grinned and motioned for him to come inside.

"And Sam," he continued, "I don't want anyone to know my wife's whereabouts."

"Of course."

"If that man calls again—"

"Don't worry, I know what to do. I'll handle

him and find out what his interests are."

The confidence in the attorney's voice relieved Adam. Breathing a little easier, he ended the call and paced the porch. What did that man want with Yasmeen? Did he know her personally, or did he recognize her last name and made the connection to Fadi? No one could touch her here. They had protection and laws in this country, damn it.

He heard tapping on the window behind him and turned around. Yasmeen motioned for him to come inside again. He lifted his index finger in the air, indicating he needed a minute. If anyone dared to set foot on his land to get to Yasmeen, he would be ready. She belonged with him. Glancing at the barn, he made a mental note to fetch his rifle after everyone left. He was probably overreacting. Let the attorney handle it for now.

He dialed Jonathan's number and told him what happened. As expected, Jonathan offered to write a letter, and volunteered Amy to do the same. Exhaling in cautious relief, he opened the door and entered the kitchen.

"Dinner will be ready in a couple of minutes," Yasmeen announced, her cheeks rosy from working near the stove. Her eyes sparkled with energy and excitement. "Will you help me set the table?"

"Sure."

"I'll get the girls ready." Lisa walked out of the kitchen.

Yasmeen stirred something green into a pot. Adam approached and stood behind her. Sweat dampened the hair covering her nape. The aromatic mixture of whatever herbs she used and her flowery scent beckoned him closer. He looked over her shoulder.

"What's for dinner?"

"You can't go wrong with spaghetti for little ones."

"Smells great."

"Wait until you taste what we . . ."

He leaned in until his chest touched her back.

Yasmeen's hand slowed. "We prepared for the adults."

Adam brought his head down to rest his chin on her shoulder, dragging his cool cheek along her warm one. "Something special?"

"Roasted chicken. My mother's recipe." Her voice was low, intimate. "You will love it."

"I love you."

Yasmeen dropped the spoon. Red sauce splashed over the white counter, some droplets landing on her face. They backed away from each other.

Lisa's annoying voice announced that Fred was

washing up for dinner. Emma and Julie ran to the table and shrieked in unison, "Spaghetti!"

Everyone stared at a red-dotted Yasmeen. The girls burst out laughing. He snatched a kitchen towel, ran it under cold water and handed it to her. "Sorry, does it hurt?" She shook her head and wiped her face, missing some spots. In the background, Lisa moved to scoop food into serving dishes. He took the towel from Yasmeen and dabbed gently at the missed spots. She stood motionless, her eyes locked on his

"You alright?"

She whispered back, "Are you sorry?"

He lowered his hand. "Only about the timing."

Fred walked in and took the chair at the head of the table. "Are we eatin', or what? I'm starvin'."

***

Dazed and thrown off balance, Yasmeen sat in silence. She wished to be alone to absorb what happened. How could three simple words make her dance inside while her body sat still? Did he know what she was going through? She sat across from Adam like a statue. How could he? The candleholder in the middle of the table obstructed part of his face. She leaned to one side, pretending to adjust her chair. Did he mean it? What made him say it now, in the middle of all this chaos? Was he trying to prove something to his father? Was he afraid she might tell Fred the truth about their marriage and embarrass him?

Fred bowed his head and launched into prayer, holding hands with his wife and daughters. Adam kept his hands in his lap, and his eyes on hers.

Everyone ate.

Everyone else.

Yasmeen moved her food around on her plate. They laughed, fake laughter, a bit too loud and misplaced in her opinion. She pretended to follow their conversation. Adam had looked surprised when he said *he loved her*. Was it a reaction to the emotional mess he was in because of his father?

"So, what sort of name is Yasmeen? Where are you from?" Fred talked with food in his mouth, the pronunciation of her name correct but distorted.

"Turkey." Adam answered on her behalf, surprising her with his fabrication.

Julie giggled. "That's a bird."

"It's also the name of a country, honey. Far, far away." Fred pointed with his fork back and forth between Yasmeen and Adam. "How'd you guys meet?"

"Internet." Adam took a drink from his water

glass.

Why was he making things up about her background?

"Like one of those matchmaking sites?" Lisa sounded excited about the idea. "Tell me about your country, is it one of those volatile places in the Middle East?"

One question after another, Yasmeen answered Lisa's questions about Turkish culture and history, coming up with solid facts. Running out of information, she changed the subject.

"We would like to invite you to spend the night here."

"That'd be great." Lisa's face betrayed her relief.

Fred dropped his fork on his plate. "That's somethin'. Gettin' invited to my own fuckin' house."

"Watch your language, Fred." Adam's tone sounded threatening. "You should be thankful for my wife's generosity."

"Oh, but we are." Lisa touched Yasmeen's arm. "Thank you."

Yasmeen didn't know what to say, Adam watchful of her every move, making her nervous and confused about how to act.

Fred shoved his plate forward. "You never told

me how you hurt your leg."

"Don't be nosy," Lisa rushed in. "I'm sure if he wanted to talk about it, he would."

"What's it to you? I'm talkin' to my son here."

Yasmeen watched for Lisa's reaction, expecting her to tell Fred not to use that demeaning tone with her. But Lisa pursed her lips, brought her head down, and twirled noodles around her fork. Frustrated, Yasmeen sought Adam. He scowled at Fred with blatant hatred in his eyes, jaw clenched, shoulders squared. Searching for a way to alleviate the tension, she reached for the water pitcher and filled Lisa's glass.

Fred tilted his head toward Adam. "That old tractor, huh? Ran over your leg?"

Adam remained quiet, his face turned to stone. She waited for him to correct Fred about the cause of his injury. Nothing. Not a sound, or a blink. Was he even breathing? She opened her mouth. Adam moved his head from side to side, the movement almost invisible. She pretended to wipe her lips with her napkin.

Fred pointed a finger at Adam, addressing Yasmeen. "Did you know your husband had a difficult time learnin' how to control the old monster?" He let out a loud, long burp.

Emma and Julie laughed and fanned their faces.

"Had to teach him the hard way," Fred bellowed through another burp.

"I remember." Adam's voice came out strange, disturbing. "Those teaching sessions are impossible to forget."

The muscles of Yasmeen's abdomen tightened with dread. What was going on here? She pressed a hand to her stomach.

Fred held his knife, ran its blade slowly through the candle flame. "The old monster overpowered you, huh?"

Something spread over Fred's face. Not a smile. Not a smirk. A sinister look Yasmeen had seen before, on faces she longed to forget, spewing poison when they opened their mouths. Her stomach lurched its contents to her throat.

The look in Adam's eyes turned cold. Distant. Sweat glistened on his forehead.

Back and forth, the blade cut through the flame. "Seems we were a few lessons short."

With the agility of a wild cat, Adam snatched the knife out of Fred's hand and sent it flying into the kitchen sink. "Learned a few things on my own, old man."

The girls clasped their hands. "Again, again," they cheered.

Fred placed his hands flat on the table, inflated

his chest. "I see."

Adam held his stare. "For everyone's sake, I hope you do." He shoved his chair back with enough force, it crashed to the floor when he left it. Adam didn't look back. He went to the kitchen sink, splashed his face with water.

Lisa ushered the girls into the downstairs bathroom, leaving a trail of sticky noodles on the floor.

Yasmeen waited until the girls were out of earshot. "Don't play with fire, Fred. You will not like the outcome."

"Yeah? And what would that be?" His tone filled with content.

"With my background? Anything is possible. Use your imagination."

Fred sprang to his feet. "You threatnin' me, bitch?"

Adam swung around from the sink. "I'd watch it if I were you. She can use a gun."

Yasmeen blinked. Why did Adam say that? She did not intend for this conversation to reach this point. Or did she? She watched him, standing at full attention, facing his father. Years of anguish etched in his rigid body. Buried vulnerability seeped from deep within, hung around his eyes and hit her full force. Would she fire a weapon to protect Adam from this monster? Yes. She would. She returned her gaze to Fred. To her surprise, Fred's lips spread in a wide smile.

"Well, I'll be. You got yourself a fighter, son."

Adam held his stance. Didn't utter a sound.

Repulsed by sitting in close proximity to Fred, she grabbed her plate and left the table.

"My turn." Adam took the plate from her hand. "You cooked, I'll clean up." A strange expression lingered on his face. Doubt? Did he suspect she was alarmed by what transpired? How could she show him she grasped the full depth of his anguish? That she didn't feel threatened by the violence it spurred? That he didn't have to suffer Fred's taunting alone? She held Adam's wrist and gave it a gentle squeeze. Leaning in sideways, she wrapped her arms around his waist, giving him a full hug. Did he get her hint? Did he understand she wasn't afraid of him?

"Let the women do their jobs. Join me downstairs." Fred headed to the basement, mumbling something about a nice surprise for his daughters.

Adam exhaled. "Jerk."

"He will be out of here in the morning. I am going upstairs. The children will probably sleep soon, and the beds need to be prepared."

"I'll come help you soon as I'm done."

While washing dishes, Adam's cell vibrated on the kitchen counter. He snatched it just in time before it fell off the edge. Sam's voice greeted him again.

"What is it?" He headed outside.

"Not sure how to tell you."

He jogged to the barn, escaping freezing wind. Good thing Sam didn't call on the landline. "Just say it."

"Al Afandy called again. Said he was using a private cell phone, not one issued by the embassy to its staff."

"What the hell does this guy want?" He crowded his body into Earnest's stall. He used the horse's body heat to stay warm.

"Al Afandy said he knew Miss Jabir's brother, Fadi."

"Shit. I was afraid of that."

"He claimed they graduated together from college. Wanted to know if his friend's sister was alright. If she needed anything."

"You believe him?"

"Didn't at first. But he insisted he didn't want to know where Miss Jabir is, or anything like that. Said he would only communicate with me should she need his services." Sam paused. "Don't know what to tell you. The guy sounded sincere."

He ran his hand down the horse's neck. "I don't like this. Don't like it one bit."

"Al Afandy explained he was trapped working at the embassy. Can't quit and disappear without protection, so he's staying in his position until he found a safe way to leave the embassy. Does whatever he can to help his friends and their families in the meantime."

Sam had more to add, but something held him back. "What else?"

"He wanted to know if Miss Jabir was alone here."

"Did you tell him?"

The attorney breathed into the phone. "I told him she was well taken care of by her husband."

"Damn it, Sam." Adam couldn't control his anger. "We agreed you wouldn't say anything."

"Calm down. Listen, if this guy isn't upfront with us, then it's better he knows your wife has people here to protect her. I didn't mention your name."

"He can easily find out. Public records."

"I doubt he'll make trouble. His reaction was a bit … surprising."

Adam leaned his back to the stall's sidewall, apprehension making his mouth dry. "How?"

"He asked if you were a good man."

"Yeah?"

"He said, and I quote, Yasmeen deserves the best."

***

In the middle of the hallway, Yasmeen struggled to concentrate. How was she going to do this? She took a deep breath and walked into her room. Moving fast, she got to work, hoping to be done with her plan before Lisa or Fred showed up. While she had her head buried in her closet, Adam's hand grabbed her shoulder. "What're you doing?"

She pulled back and dumped a bundle of clothes in his hands. "Good, you are here. Quick, take these to your mother's room."

"Why?"

"I don't have time to explain, just do it." She ushered him to the hallway. "Throw them in the closet. Take your clothes and things too. I will change the sheets here."

Adam moved as instructed. He made several trips to clear his closet. Yasmeen entered his mother's room with a stack of clean linens in her hands.

"What are they doing downstairs?" She was out of breath from working fast.

"I left them going through family albums Fred found in the basement."

"That should keep them busy. We are almost done here. Did you take most of your personal things out of your room? Including what is in your drawers?" She stripped the cover off the bed.

"Yup." He pointed at the pile he created in one corner. "What's going on?" He helped her spread clean sheets over the mattress.

"The girls will sleep in your room. Fred and Lisa will take my room." She straightened and faced him across the bed. "You and I will sleep here."

His hands let go of the sheet. A quick burst of air escaped his lungs.

"I know it's only for one night, but I didn't think you would want Lisa to sleep in your mother's bed." She smoothed her hand over the sheet. "Or Fred, for that matter. It only makes sense to give them the guest bedroom and give your bed to your sisters." She bit her lower lip. "Unless you think of a better arrangement?"

"The arrangement's perfect."

CHAPTER 30

A GHOST

The house quieted down after everyone disappeared into their designated rooms. Adam remained downstairs enjoying the silence. When Fred found out he didn't have to sleep in his old room, a look of relief swept over his face. How convenient, for Fred to turn his back on the past like that and shove it all aside. Take another room. Create another family. Look through old pictures and see only the smiles, few as they were.

Adam roamed through the house, switching off lights, careful to step around scattered things the kids left on the floor. He examined the gas stove knobs as usual, returned the phone handset to its base, made sure the fire died in the fireplace, and locked the doors.

Facing the windows in the living room, he stood in the dark, hands in his pockets, buying some time. Yasmeen waited for him upstairs. She must be a nervous wreck. Hell, he was in no better shape. He shouldn't have told her he loved her, not like that.

Not then. Not while she saw him suffer Fred's presence like a frightened boy. And she came to his defense, threatened Fred out right to his face, gave Adam a hug when he least expected it. Did she mean it? Or was it part of her pretense in front of Fred? The smart woman made sure Fred didn't suspect anything was off in this marriage, setting up the rooms like that. Saved him a great deal of face.

An owl hooted outside. He placed his hands on the windowsill, leaned forward and bent his knee repeatedly. His leg ached, reminding him of the day's events. He shouldn't have done a lot of things. Pamela Phelps. He shook his head. Why the hell didn't he just walk out of the store? And what was Yasmeen thinking in Ben's truck, touching him like that? Was that an invitation?

He straightened and ran a hand through his hair. He couldn't touch her tonight. Not before he knew what she wanted, not when his head was screwed up like this. He sighed in frustration.

"God damn you, Fred Shipman." His words cut through the silence around him. He wished the man was awake to hear them.

Checking the time on his watch, he decided he had given Yasmeen enough time to get ready and dress for bed. So, she would share a bed with him tonight. Forced, more like it, because his father wanted to make amends. The man waited fifteen long years, he couldn't wait one more fucking day?

Resigned to take control of the situation, he headed upstairs. The only light came from under the door of his mother's room, guiding him through the dark quiet hallway. He went into the bathroom and washed, making sure he made enough noise for Yasmeen to hear him. In front of his mother's room, he coughed twice, counted to ten, opened the door and walked in.

Yasmeen faced the door, her back to the window. She wore the black robe with the lavender satin bow, her hair damp and brushed back. The night lamps on each side of the bed cast strange shadows on her face.

"It's freezing in here." He closed the door, careful not to let it slam.

"Is it always cold in this room?" Yasmeen's voice sounded strained and unnatural.

"Nope."

He went to the corner opposite where she stood, kneeled with difficulty by the pile of clothes on the floor, and shifted some aside. Warm air blew in.

"Heater vent was blocked. I was in such a hurry when I brought my stuff, didn't pay attention where I dropped them." He straightened. Yasmeen's cheeks were pale, her hands clasped in front of her, and her body trembled.

"Come here."

She unclasped her hands but didn't move her feet.

"It's warmer by the heater vent." He hoped he sounded calm and collected.

Taking slow steps, she came forward. The panels of her robe parted with her steps, revealing the lavender nightgown, smooth, simple and tight around her waist. Her flowery scent crowded his senses. He took a couple of steps to the side, maintaining some distance between them.

"Thank you."

"For what?" She extended her hands to the warm draft.

"For all that you did today. I know it wasn't easy."

She shrugged.

"Especially with the way I behaved earlier."

The hem of her robe fluttered over the vent. "I know the day was difficult for you too. What do they call it, when things go up and down like that? That fast ride in the amusement park?"

"A roller coaster." His eyes concentrated on the dancing material around her knees. He took another step back. Looking for her reaction, he posed the question he'd been wanting to ask for quite a while now. "Does the name Haytham Al Afandy ring a bell?"

She frowned. "I don't hear the doorbell."

"No, Yasmeen. I meant do you know anyone by that name? Haytham Al Afandy?"

"Umm, no. Why? Who is he?"

"He works at the Syrian Embassy, I think. He called Sam asking to talk to you."

"Al Afandy," she sounded the name again. "It's a big family, well known." She gasped. "Wait, I think he is one of Fadi's friends. He didn't come to our house often. Maybe he has news about my father?"

"Sam will find out what he wanted and let me know."

Adam picked at his clothes on the floor for sheer pretense. Could this Al Afandy character be as benign as a secret admirer, nothing else? He pulled a tee-shirt out. Better know more about this guy. He turned his back to her, unbuttoned his shirt and took it off.

"Did you watch the news today? I didn't have a chance." Her voice had dropped a few decibels.

He shoved his arms in the sleeves, angry at himself for starting something he couldn't finish. She looked for information. About Al Afandy? Not likely. The name didn't faze her. She didn't flinch or anything when she heard it. He turned to face her again. "Nothing new. Sorry."

Yasmeen held a pair of his pajama pants in her hand. She handed them over and moved to sit on the chest at the foot of the bed. "Why did you tell Fred I'm Turkish?"

"I don't trust him." He kept the pajama pants in his hands.

"What could he do if he knew the truth?" She had that innocent look on her face. "I mean that I am from Syria. I don't think it would make any difference to him. In his eyes, I am a foreigner either way."

He snapped the pajama pants in the air, pretending to straighten them. "You don't know Fred as well as I do."

"I don't understand."

"He'll do whatever it takes to put me back under his control."

"What could he do to you now? You are a grown man."

Tapping his leg with the pants, he studied Yasmeen, her bare feet barely touching the floor. Oblivious and fragile, no matter what she thought of herself. All it took was a phone call from Fred to anyone looking for her, like that Al Afandy guy.

"He'll use you to hurt me. I'm not about to give

him any ammunition. Fred doesn't need to know about your real background, and that's final." He didn't mean to sound intimidating, but she flinched. He ground his teeth. Shit, now he sounded like his old man.

"Don't let him get to you like that." She ambled toward him, coming within his reach.

"Can't help it. Sorry. I'm a little on edge. It's been a long day. We both need some shuteye." Draping his pajama pants over his shoulder, he passed her to grab one pillow off the bed and returned to the clothes pile. "I'll sleep here." He threw the pillow down and fumbled with his belt.

"You need a blanket."

"I'm fine. It's warm enough near the vent." He unzipped his pants.

"Do you need the light?"

"Nope." He waited until she turned off both nightlights. He changed pants and stretched on his back. Although he couldn't see anything, he closed his eyes anyway, and crossed his arms on his forehead. It sounded like she removed her robe, and then slipped between the sheets.

Several minutes passed.

"Adam?"

"Hmmm."

"Do you believe in ghosts?"

"Why do you ask?"

She remained silent.

"Yasmeen?"

"I just wanted to know your view. Do you?"

"Nope."

She sighed.

He lowered his arms to his sides. "Are you . . . sensing . . . a presence?"

"I don't think ghosts waste their time with the living. Goodnight."

The sheets rustled, and he imagined her flipping to one side. A bundle under him pushed against his lower back. He shifted his weight and smoothed it as much as he could. His bare heels rested on the hardwood floor. Bending his knees, he dragged a piece of clothing under his feet and stretched. Something cold and hard poked his thigh. He suppressed a curse, pulled the metal thing out, scraping the wood.

"Are you alright?"

"My belt buckle, sorry. Go to sleep." His chest constricted as if he had been running, the nerves in his body on full alert, aware of nature's pull toward soft, warm Yasmeen. He tried to relax and bring his heart rate down.

"Adam?"

His pulse spiked. He loved the foreign way she

said his name, pronouncing the d with clarity. "What now?"

"If it's not superstition about your mother's bed that is keeping you away from it, what is?"

In one heartbeat, he sprang to his feet and turned on the nightlight.

Yasmeen sat in bed, rested her back on the headboard, keeping her legs straight. Her hands clutched the edge of the comforter to her chest.

"I meant what I said in the kitchen. It wasn't a mistake. I want you to know that." He came closer. "Should've chosen a better moment to tell you, but that's how it happened. I don't want you to go. I'll try to bring your mother here if you want. Or I'll go with you to visit, if you insist on leaving to see her. Either way, I want to be with you." He placed his hand on his chest. "The only reason that's keeping me away from this bed, is that I don't know how you feel about me." Could he be any clearer? He let his hand fall to his side. Was his timing off again? Did he say too much?

Yasmeen reached for his hand. "Join me, Adam."

THE END

Acknowledgements

My greatest gratitude is for my true friend, husband and loving father of my children, Saad Saleh. His unwavering support guided me through difficult times of doubt and hesitation to write this story.

I am indebted to the following for their expert advice, assistance and encouragement:

My children, Leila and Bassel, for questioning almost everything I say, trying to keep me focused.

My parents, Hasan and Nawal, for being transparent, and for letting me know what works and what doesn't.

My brother, Basel Taha, for remaining a constant force behind my back, pushing me forward.

My best friend, Manal Broeckelmann, for her solid belief in my writing ability, and for dragging me to my first writing critique group session.

Roger Paulding, for showing me the skills on how to write a story, and not just tell one.

Chris Hernandez, for sharing his expertise as a war veteran.

Sharon Dotson, for her encouragement and endless channeling of information.

My colleagues at the Writers Critique Group, for allowing me to use their valuable input and comments to improve my writing, specifically, Luke Chauvin and Barbara Andrews.